AGING OUT

AGING OUT

L. Lee Shaw

Boho
Books
MOLALLA, OR

This is a work of fiction. All of the characters, organizations, and events portrayed in this novel are either products of the author's imagination or are used fictionally.

AGING OUT
Copyright © 2017 by L. Lee Shaw

ISBN: 978-0-9988455-0-0 (paperback)
        978-0-9988455-1-7 (ebook)

Printed in the United States of America

Boho Books paperback edition / October 2017

To Emily, Mary, and Bert—sweet ladies from long ago who still live in the attic of my memory.

CONTENTS

ADAM RIDDICK

PH Case No. 2013-3-26

Yeah, I know it's stupid, but pretty much all I ever wanted was somebody to give a rat's ass that I was sucking air and walking around—you know, notice I actually existed.

Conceived to cement my mom's then relationship, I morphed into a means of revenge when things went south. The problem with that move was then *she* was stuck with me. Since it wasn't politically correct to put a two-year-old out to fend for himself, she did her best to ignore my existence for the next thirteen years. We ended up living with her mother, Velma, who loathed both the idea of being a grandmother and me for daily reminding her of it. Eventually, it was decided I had way overstayed my welcome. So at fifteen I was dumped on the street along with the other garbage.

After being spotted hanging at a location not usually frequented by teenagers at four in the morning, I was placed in Pittison House, the local prep school for the totally pathetic.

My first two years, every other kid came and went. I shoulda felt like a moldy crust in the back of the drawer, unnoticed and for sure unwanted, but that pretty much summed up my life anyway.

When Soosie was placed, my reign as champion in the sullen, noncommunicative division was over. Rumor had it she was here because she tried to kill someone. Since most everything you hear in this place is usually coming out of the mouth of some idiot looking to work his way up the Pitt's food chain, I blew it off.

I should have taken it as an omen when my old haunted dream showed up after a long absence.

It's night. It's raining. I am walking along a lit street. The longer I walk, the farther apart the streetlights are, until I walk past the last one and all I can see is endless darkness waiting to swallow me.

This is usually the point I wake up with my heart jackhammering in my chest. Tonight was no different. I lay awake for a long time, so I had a late start in the morning, which meant I wasn't jockeying for position at the urinals for a change. In fact, the only person in the bathroom was a guy hanging up a towel.

I admit it. I gawked as he carefully aligned the edges. I think that was one of the few occasions in my extended time in the Pitt the towels were anywhere but on the floor.

Although I seldom bothered to learn anyone's name because so many were gone before I find any reason to speak to them, this guy's name carried a certain aroma in Soda Springs, so it stuck with me.

Despite the town's prevailing opinion of his family, he was very quiet and neat, even if he didn't dress down to the usual standards around here. He did have a way of freaking people out with his over-the-top politeness. "Yes, sir." "No, ma'am." Never cursed. I mean, some pierced, permanently painted thug calling you twelve different pornographic names is the usual morning ride to breakfast. Some guy saying, "Excuse me, please go first" was just wrong in this place.

I spent a couple extra minutes in the bathroom finger-combing my hair so Mr. Clean Jeans could have a head start because another really annoying thing about him was he actually acknowledged you. Me, I understood my function in life was to be ignored, and that just totally messed with my program.

I don't know why the guy wasn't already gone when I wandered out, but he was still hanging on the landing at the top of the stairs when Soosie's combat boots stomped into view.

Honestly, all the guy did was step aside and silently gesture for her to go ahead.

The chick flipped. She grabbed him by his shirt and slammed him up against the wall in less than a heartbeat. "Don't you disrespect me, Tatum." Her anger charged the air. "You ever so much as even look my direction, and I'm going to gut you."

Great, still another fight in the hallowed halls of the Pitt happening between where I was and where I wanted to be. I edged my way around the two, inadvertently glancing into the guy's eyes. Something there pinched me in a place that felt uncomfortably familiar.

I answered by sucking it in to squeeze past Soosie just as she whipped something out of her back pocket and flung her arm back to take a good swing with it.

Stupidly, I grabbed her arm. And bada-bing, Tatum was a freed man and I had the ass end of a rattail comb looking to poke unnecessary holes in my body.

Maybe the rumor mill wasn't so far off this time.

SOOSIE FRETWELL

PH Case No. 2016-1-14

The voice in my head was booming furious. *Girl, are you some kind of stupid or what? This place is your only chance to get clear of the mess you made when you beat the crap out of your sister, and you just about frickin' blew it this morning! Get a grip, dumb butt!*

It didn't matter I could justify things by saying if she hadn't done what she did, I wouldn't have done what I did, but the truth is I probably would have done it eventually anyway.

The only satisfaction I had when they hauled me away hooked up in the back of a squad car was that Sammy would be safe. Oh, and my sister was already on her way to jail.

Lucky for me, the court determined there were "mitigating" circumstances and took the DA's recommendation for diversion, so I got packed off to Pittison House instead of juvie jail.

But then, just to show how freakin' warped life really is, I end up at the same place as a relative of the family who supersized the screwed mess that had been my life.

Now here I am, sitting outside the room mothers' office door, waiting for some exciting announcement they want to share with me. Don't know why they couldn't have shared it when they were chewing me a new one this morning. I mean, seriously, when is it a big offense to take out a Tatum? It should earn you a Congressional Medal of Honor or something.

Really? As if my day couldn't get shittier, here comes that loser Riddick.

I hate the guy. He's always staring off into space like he's above us all or something. You think he's looking at you, but if you look really close, you realize there's barely enough intelligence under all those blonde waves to keep the pilot light flickering. Yeah, drop your tall, blonde, and stupid ass in a chair while I forget you exist.

Muddertrucker! Is Tatum slithering into the room, too? Geez, just kill me now.

MYRON TATUM

PH Case No. 2015-10-2

T errific. I was told to show up for some kind of announcement at ten, and who's waiting here? That whacked chick
who wants to waste me for being a Tatum.

I'm sorry, but I didn't really get a lot of say in the matter. If you
people think it's hard living around Tatums, you should try being
a Tatum. Try walking around all the time waiting for someone to
jump in your face over something that happened before you were
even hatched just because of your last name.

Sometimes I just want to stand on the tallest building in town
and scream, "I didn't do it!"

'Course, a lot of good it would do me. It didn't do me any
good when they decided out of the whole student body that I,
and I alone, had the skills to hack the school computer and mess
with grades. Even when it was established that at the time of the
dastardly deed, I was hoisting Great-Great-Uncle Trey's body into
the back of a hearse in front of about hundred people who had
come to see if Great-Great-Aunt Verna's prophecy he would one
day drink himself to death had actually come to pass. They were
delighted to know at age eighty nine, he had fulfilled her dire
warning. Actually, Trey had drunk like a flippin' fish for about
eight decades before it caught up with him. Whatever else the
Tatums may lack, a titanium liver is not one of them.

7

The school dismissed it as being "irrelevant."

Right—over a hundred witnesses, including the preacher and funeral home director who, for the record, are not related to any of us, were irrelevant.

So going to Plan B, I asked them what my motive would be since I was a four-point student. They didn't have an answer, so they conveniently ignored it before suspending me out of school.

Luckily, the early release let me arrive home just in time to see them hauling Dad out of the house in handcuffs, and, yup, right on cue, the medics were carrying Mom in a transport chair while she hollered at them to grab the bottle off the table. It was the usual drill.

The police chief came up when he saw me. He's always been decent to me. I think he kinda feels sorry for me. And yeah, that makes two of us. "Go pack your stuff, Myron. I'll drop you at your grandma's." It was also part of the drill, except this time it was different. I explained Grandma Weaver had had a stroke in the spring and was now in an assisted living facility.

He was left scratching his head. After taking me down to sit around the police station for a few hours, the only place they could find for me was here at the Pitt.

Chief Braden apologized when he drove me over. "Sorry about this, Myron, but you are technically under the state's protection now, and I'm pretty sure leaving you with any of your other family would be a violation of some state law."

I couldn't argue.

So here I stand while Ms. Psycho decides how best to off me.

Look, girl, I'm related to about a gazillion outlaws. I don't know who did what to whom, and I'm sorry, but there is nothing I can do about it because *I didn't do it!*

Chapter 1

The office door opened. Dustin, the daytime house counselor, motioned to the teens. Although Myron stood back a respectful distance, Soosie's trajectory careened in his direction.

"Soosie, Pitt is an option for you. But, as we discussed earlier, it is not the only option." There was an implicit warning in Dustin's voice. She took an awkward side step to put distance between herself and Myron.

Only after she passed Dustin and was inside the room did Adam and Myron follow.

Soosie flung herself onto the couch and crossed her arms and legs while she glowered at the men. Adam claimed the easy chair.

Since the rest of the room was filled with two desks, several filing cabinets, and a bookcase, remaining seating options were limited. Myron stopped just inside the door and looked around uncertainly before carefully edging himself around to stand in the few square feet of floor space furthest from the couch and its occupant.

After riffling through papers on his desk, Dustin swung his office chair around. "All three of you are slated to age out of Pittison in the next six months. Under state law, our obligation to provide care for you will be terminated, and we will dump you in the streets." He looked at the three kids. "Frankly, that rubs us wrong. So to give you some way to sustain yourselves after we yank the safety net, you are being given an opportunity to work. This will provide both some money and real life experience to help in your transition.

"Beginning Monday at 7:00 a.m., the three of you will report to Elena Fuentes at Soda Springs Care Center, where you will be taking on housekeeping and laundry duties."

Soosie's sharp inhalation drew everyone's attention. Alarm was evident on her face.

"Something wrong, Soosie?" Dustin asked.

Her face immediately resumed its perpetual scowl as she shook her head and drew tighter into herself.

Watching from the corner of his eye, Myron recognized something new was drifting in the air. It felt like apprehension—and it was coming from Soosie.

"So here's how it's gonna work. We have passes we will give you Monday morning for the bus running two blocks down on Main Street. Your shift is from 7:00 a.m. to 3:30 p.m. You will be expected to report back here at 4:15.

"You will conduct yourselves appropriately and you will do your job. Whatever problem you think you have with each other is to be left by the front door when you go out it. Whether you like each other or not is irrelevant to us. The care center is willing to give you a chance you desperately need, and we do not want it screwed up because of bull crap, got it? Any questions?"

Silence answered.

Chapter 2

At 6:20 a.m. on the following Monday, Adam, Soosie, and Myron stood at the Pitt's front door. Dustin did a silent inspection before handing out the bus passes. "Mrs. Fuentes assured me the nursing center would be providing your lunches and break snacks," he said. "You are to behave appropriately, do your job, and no trouble, got it?"

He entered the code that disabled the house alarm and opened the door. The teens remained immobile, staring out at the early morning sky framed in the open door.

"The zombies are all tucked into bed now, so move your butts," Dustin commanded.

Goosed by his words, three Pitties straggled out the door.

It was an awkward walk to the bus stop. In trying to keep distance between himself and Soosie, Myron ended up having to sprint the last few yards to make the bus.

They climbed off at the corner of Third and Fir. The care center stood catercorner. Lights were visible through the front windows overlooking the wide front porch.

Drawing a deep breath, Myron stepped off the curb and crossed the empty street. After a moment, Soosie and Adam followed.

Soda Springs Care Center had begun life as a big, square, two-story family home. Over the decades, it morphed from family to institution. Additions included a one-level cement block wing on the right side of the house parallel to the sidewalk. A similar addition jutted out of the back and ended at the alley running through the middle of the block. The left side of the original house accommodated a long wheelchair ramp angled from the veranda-style front porch to the sidewalk.

Stopping at the bottom of the steps, the trio looked up at the door. Unconsciously, they climbed the steps in sync and paused when they reached the porch.

Focused on the door, all three jumped when a voice near the wheelchair ramp spoke.

"Hey, kids. Any of you spot a witch hanging around over there?" The question flowed to them on a cloud of cigar smoke.

Looking in the direction of the voice, they saw a man in an electric wheelchair seated in the remaining shadows, the end of his cigar glowing red as he drew on it.

Exchanging uncertain looks, Myron answered. "Ah, no, sir. There was no one at the bus stop."

The man grunted. "Probably still making breakfast for the flying monkeys." The cigar glowed again.

The odd exchange pushed the three to punch the large square entry button beside the door. When it swung open, they crossed into the smell of disinfectant and old age.

A few feet inside the room, a table lamp illuminated a large desk appearing to serve as a reception counter. There was no one in sight, although they could hear voices and sounds coming from the back of the center. The empty hallway to their right was dimly lit.

The trio looked around cautiously as they waited.

A small enclosed room with a closed door occupied a corner of the larger room. The rest of the area opened into a space with several retro Formica-topped tables surrounded by an unmatched assortment of chairs. Two vinyl-covered recliners, their arms patched with duct tape, and a loveseat were pushed up against a wall. An entertainment unit housing a large flat-screen TV stood opposite. Stacks of DVDs were piled on its shelves. Although everything was tidy, there was a tired shabbiness to both the furnishings and the room.

But what caught their attention were huge, garish abstract paintings covering much of the walls. The incongruity of the art and its setting gave a weird vibe to the space.

The door behind them swooshed open, and the man who had spoken to them on the porch rolled in. The three instinctively huddled a little closer to each other.

He wheeled over to the desk, where he pitched the stub of his cigar into a wastebasket. Turning his chair, he leaned back to look up at them with bright curiosity through the thick lenses of his glasses.

As he studied them, his wiry gray-white eyebrows drew together. "Is she all right?" he asked.

Soosie was swaying slightly, and a tinge of green edged her pale face. The smell of the facility had sucked the air out of her as it overwhelmed with memories of life exploding and slinging destruction in every direction.

Turning, Myron reached out to touch her arm. "Soos?"

His gesture gave her something to push against emotionally, and in a moment, color flooded her face.

"I'm fine," she said through clenched teeth.

"So, you kids selling something or collecting for some cause?"

"Ah, no, sir. We're from Pittison House. We're supposed to meet with Mrs. Fuentes to start working today," Myron answered.

"So you're the replacements."

"Are you Mr. Fuentes?" Myron asked.

"Nah. He's short and has an accent. I'm one of the old guys from down the hall. When I taught school, I was Mr. Hirsch. Around here I'm just David. What're your names?"

The teens shifted their weights, looking at each other out of the corner of their eyes.

"What? Are you in a witness protection program or something? Okay, how about this. I point and you tell." He pointed to Soosie. "Sorry, gents, but I always start with the pretty ones. It's a good rule to live by." He waited expectantly.

"Soosie." Her voice came out small and reluctant.

The man's tone was gentle. "Soosie what?"

"Soosie Fretwell."

"Your dad Sam?"

She answered by avoiding the man's eyes.

"I knew your dad. He was one of my students in the long ago. I'm very sorry."

Soosie abruptly turned away.

The man watched her for a silent moment before pointing to Myron. "How about you?"

"Myron, sir." Myron jutted his chin out slightly and stiffened his back. "Myron Tatum, sir."

"You Vernon's boy or Ralph's?"

"Vernon's, sir."

"You have my sympathy, son."

Myron dipped his chin in acknowledgment.

The man turned his attention to Adam.

"You look familiar. Real familiar. What's your name?"

"Adam…Adam Riddick."

"Do I know your family?"

"Doubt it," Adam answered.

"Are you sure?" the man asked curiously.

"Pretty sure. My mom's not from around here."

"What about your dad?"

Adam leveled his blue eyes at the man before shaking his head. There was a hard set to his jaw. "I don't know who my dad is."

The man studied Adam for a moment more. Then he pointed at each of them again. "Soosie, Myron, Adam. Of course, this is not saying I won't get your names confused later. Used to be I could remember every student in my classes just by going around the room one time and having them tell me their names. We're talking upwards of twenty-five kids times five classes. Now I gotta find my wallet some days just to remember *my* name."

The man maneuvered his wheelchair close to the desk and began to pound on a hotel call bell. "You gotta make noise if you want to get any action in this place."

A very pregnant Latina woman balancing a pile of folded towels in her arms emerged from the hall at the back of the room.

Her progress to the desk was followed by a querulous voice. "Angie? Angie, it's not in the closet, and I can't find it anywhere." A short, skinny person steadily shuffled a walker in her wake.

The kids goggled when the determined advance stopped next to the desk. The person was wearing a vintage nylon blouse translucent enough to reveal the lacy top of the full slip underneath. But the person's white hair was buzz cut, and stubble sprouted from his cheeks and chin.

"What's a matter, Paul? Somebody kipe your girdle again?" David asked.

15

The man cast a disdainful look. "Anyone who lives in sweats is in no position to comment on other people's fashion choices."

"Please tell me you can find what he wants to wear," David said to the young woman. "Or we will all be subjected to still another dramatic recitation on the shortcomings of the laundry room at breakfast, lunch, and dinner. And speaking of the laundry room, these are the kids from Pittison. Soosie, Myron, and Adam," he said pointing them out. With that, David backed up and full-throttled his wheelchair toward the back hall.

Ignoring the kids, Paul turned his attention back to the woman. "Angie, I can't find my yellow polka-dotted skirt. I want to wear it today."

"It is in the laundry, Paulie. You wore it the day before yesterday to Emily's birthday party and got chocolate ice cream on it. I had to soak it."

Drawing his eyebrows together, the man was apparently searching his memory to verify her statement.

The lights in the hall to their right suddenly turned on, and the kids shifted their attention momentarily.

A very large woman was being wheeled out of a room and up the hall. She gabbled away while gently plucking at the ruffles festooning the skirt and sleeves of a pink, flowered muumuu. A pink play tiara, like those sold in dollar stores, sat on her snow-white curls. She looked like an immense, over-decorated cake.

The nursing aide pushing her was almost as startling. Her improbably red big hairstyle framed a heavily made-up face. The neon yellow scrubs she wore looked like they would glow in the dark, as did the matching chandelier earrings brushing her shoulders. She was cooing to the woman in honeyed tones. "Now, Miss

Bert, if you ain't about the prettiest thing today. The boys are going to be falling all over themselves trying to get you to flirt with them. I bet you are going to break all their hearts before this day is over."

The teens edged closer to the desk as she maneuvered the wheelchair around them to one of the larger dining room tables.

The man, Paul, totally ignored the activity. "Well, since all my favorite things are being held hostage in the laundry, I have absolutely no idea what I am going to wear today."

"Maybe you could borrow something from Bert," the pregnant woman said, flipping a hand in the direction of the table.

"Really, Angie, that isn't very nice. There is no way I could wear anything of Bert's. You know she has absolutely deplorable taste."

He looked the kids over. "If they are going to be doing the laundry, make sure they know my dainties are hand-washed and not run through the machines with Steve's jeans."

He and his walker stumped off.

Angie flashed the kids an apologetic smile before calling across the room. "Olivia, do you know where Elena is? The Pittison people are here."

The woman responded by pointing toward the teens. "Why, lookie there, Miss Bert. We have us some company."

The woman in the wheelchair gave them the beatific smile of a toddler before returning her attention to the table, which she was gently patting with both hands.

Hurrying over, Olivia scooped the towels out of Angie's arms. "You just take a load off, sugar, and I'll find her."

In the silence that gathered as they watched the yellow-clad woman trot down the hall to the back of the center, Myron became aware of pressure against his arm. He was startled to realize Soosie was unconsciously leaning into him.

He heard her whispering to herself. "Toto, I don't think we're in Kansas anymore."

Chapter 3

From the moment Mrs. Fuentes bustled up to greet them, the three teens found themselves being inextricably, if reluctantly, enfolded into the care center.

After being guided through the required paperwork, Mrs. Fuentes provided each of them with scrubs to work in. While the boys were given outfits in forest green and navy blue, she insisted Soosie wear rosy-pink pants with a color-matching flowered top—a far cry from the faded jeans and black hoodies she normally hid in.

After taking turns changing in the employee bathroom, they reassembled at the desk.

"Ah, that is your color, Soosie. Leave the black for old ladies," she said. "Is she not pretty?" she asked the young men.

Adam and Myron glanced at each other, trying to gauge an answer that would not put their lives at further risk when they were no longer in the safety of the care center. They settled for a quick nod as they looked anywhere but at the girl with danger sparking in her blue eyes.

The short, stocky Hispanic woman began their orientation in a large room at the back of the facility. It held four hospital beds, three of them occupied by women. She moved lightly around the room, straightening a blanket, adjusting a pillow, or patting a hand as she introduced the occupants of the beds to the teens.

Two of the women appeared to be already packed and waiting in life's exit line, as they gave no response to Elena's ministrations. Only one woman, whose curled and twisted body occupied an unnaturally small part of her bed, watched with protective eyes when Elena smoothed the blankets over the woman in the bed next to her. Suddenly she squawked, "Katie!"

Elena hurried around to her and patted her shoulder. "Katie is fine, Tilly. I'm just showing our new helpers around," she said gesturing to the young people.

The woman peered at them sharply before abruptly closing her eyes in dismissal.

Oddly, the room was not depressing. Cheery flowered curtains hung in front of the institutional window looking out over a courtyard. Each of the women was wearing a pretty pastel gown while colorful quilts rested on the beds. The tops of the night-stands were decorated with small pots of flowers and little stuffed animals. Katie's and Tilly's had several photographs as well. And unlike the main area of the center, the walls here were hung with sweet posters.

Olivia stuck her head in the room just as Elena was finishing her explanation of the cleaning and laundry requirements.

"Clarence is ready to get up."

The kids trailed after Elena as she headed back to the hall. Stopping at the first doorway, they watched as the two women expertly lifted the tall, skeletally thin man up in bed, pivoting him around to a sitting position. Elena supported him while Olivia positioned an olive-green cardiac chair beside the bed. Then, with one woman grasping him under each arm, they swiftly transferred him into the chair. Olivia pushed down on the back as Elena lifted the footrest. The two women fussed a few more moments, arranging small pillows around him before carefully tucking a bright tie-dyed quilt over him.

There was a second bed in the room that showed signs of recent use. Running water behind a closed door located at the foot of Clarence's bed identified the second occupant's whereabouts.

Olivia swung the chair around to face the door. At the sight of the three kids, the man lifted a wasted arm and wavered it in their direction. His lips contorted as he struggled to get a sound out. Finally, he was able to push the word "froop" out.

"Why, these are the people who will be replacing Angie while she's off having her baby," Olivia said. "This is Myron."

Clarence lifted his arm again. Myron stepped forward and enclosed the man's contractured hand in his own as he carefully shook it. Adam awkwardly followed suit upon his introduction. Soosie gave a small smile but remained rooted in the doorway when she was identified.

"You'll have to watch this one, Soosie," Olivia said as she began to push the chair in their direction. "We've caught him more than once chasing pretty girls down the hall."

The man responded with a grin lifting just one side of his mouth. It was accompanied by a gurgling sound that may have been laughter.

Although the doors to the next two rooms were closed, Elena identified them as belonging to Paul and David.

"Do not worry so much about trying to remember who is in what room. These will help you find the right person." She pointed to small personalized plaques beside each doorway.

"Other places just use tape for the names," Soosie commented softly.

Elena visibly shuddered. "That is just bad. It makes it like they are someone who is not to be there long. Here it is their home, and we honor it as such."

Going back through the main room, she led them down the hall of the wing running along the front of the facility.

Although there were four rooms along the hall, Elena explained the end room was currently vacant. Next to it was Bert's room. It was a massive pink overload, with every inch flowered, ruffled, and blinged out. Posters of various cartoon princesses were tacked to the walls.

The next resident door was closed. "This is Mary's room. Her sister passed away, and she is in Corvallis to settle things. She will be home, maybe this weekend."

The final door was open, but the room was unoccupied. A soft "wow" escaped from Soosie when she saw bookcases from floor to ceiling along one wall and extending under the window. The cases were filled to overflowing. There was hunger in her face as her eyes traveled over the books.

"Emily is always an early riser. She likes to take a walk each morning before breakfast, so you will meet her later."

"Soosie, these four rooms will be yours to clean. The empty room just needs to be dusted and vacuumed once a week to keep it fresh. Emily and Mary prefer to clean their own rooms, so you just need to vacuum and clean the bathrooms, unless they ask for more. Myron and Adam, you will do the men's rooms. The ladies will not mind who does the back ward."

She continued talking as she led them toward the laundry room. "The halls need to be swept and mopped daily, as does the main room. Tables and chairs need to be wiped off after breakfast and lunch."

A large man was swinging up the hall in their direction. The long, white ponytail falling halfway down his back matched his thick, white beard. Resting on top of a tee-shirt featuring a line of marching bears was a large metal peace symbol. A couple of alligator clips held up the empty lower left leg of his jeans.

Moving adroitly along on his forearm crutches, he stopped in front of them.

"This is Steve," Elena said. "He shares the room with Clarence."

He threw up the peace sign. "Welcome to Shambhala!" He then swung around them, the rubber tips of his crutches squeaking on the floor as he headed to David's door and knocked.

Behind him, a woman wearing a long skirt under a scrub top pushed a food trolley in the direction of the kitchen.

"How did our ladies do?" Elena asked her.

"Tilly and Katie ate well. Meryl...," Her voice trailed off as she shook her head.

Elena nodded and then introduced the young people. "This is Lidiya, one of our CNAs on day shift. Just like Olivia, if you have any questions, you can ask her."

Lidiya gave them a warm smile as she began to angle the trolley into the kitchen. "It will be good for this place to have some young people around."

A swampy, soap-scented atmosphere greeted them upon entering the laundry room.

Soosie was behind Adam. Pausing midway in, he did a slow sweep of the room. As he turned in her direction, Soosie was startled when a hint of a smile tugged at a corner of his mouth. He had been so tightly wound when they toured the rest of the facility, his shoulders had practically covered his ears. But now he looked…comfortable.

This guy really does have low wattage if he thinks a laundry room is some kind of cool, she thought.

Elena held up a clipboard with a sheet itemizing all of the required cleaning tasks, as she discussed the daily routine with the teens.

"You can collect the laundry as you clean. It is done after," she said. She then explained the color-coded chart identifying the day each residents' personal laundry was to be done, along with the daily order of the rest of the laundry.

She ended with a cheery smile. "It is a lot, but you can ask Olivia, Lidiya, or myself should you get confused. I will leave it to you to figure out how best to handle things. Don't forget to wear the gloves," pointing at a wall dispenser before disappearing out the door.

The kids stood for a long minute looking around the room and then at each other.

Myron finally spoke. "So how should we divvy things up? Maybe I can do Steve and Clarence's room and the ladies' room if you don't mind doing David's and Paul's rooms," he said to Adam.

Adam nodded. "Works for me."

Myron looked at Soosie. "We can do the back hall and the main room if you don't mind doing the front hall when you do the rooms up there."

Soosie shrugged her acceptance of the plan.

Hampers littered the laundry room by the time the trio had finished the cleaning. Looking around, Myron itemized them. "It looks like there's general laundry, the soiled laundry, and personal laundry."

"I'm pretty familiar with the big machines," Adam said, gesturing to the institutional-sized washer and dryer behind him. "I'll take them on."

"I don't mind soaking the soiled laundry before it's washed," Myron said. "I did a lot of it at home due to my mom's drin… er, issues."

"If you're okay with doing the personal laundry in those machines, Soosie," Adam said as he pointed to the residential-sized washer and dryer on the opposite wall, "then we should be good to go."

The two males assuming they could keep choosing which jobs they wanted incensed Soosie, but just as she was about to unleash her wrath, she realized she didn't want to wrestle the monster machines, and she most definitely did not want to deal with the soiled laundry. Snapping her mouth shut, she nodded and headed to the chart. "So who gets their laundry done today?"

* * * * *

Midafternoon, Elena appeared in the doorway of the laundry room. "I have checked, and you have done very good with the cleaning on this first day," she said, nodding approvingly.

"Ummm, Mrs. Fuentes?" Adam said.

"Please, we are family here, and family always calls me Elena, so now you must also call me Elena."

Adam gave a dubious nod. "The washing machine," he said, placing his hand on its front, "is draining pretty slow."

Elena nodded. "Yes. It is the pump. Arturo ordered the part for it," she gestured toward a cupboard in the corner of the laundry room, "but since he hurt his back and hip, I don't know when he will be able to fix it." She sighed, and this time her smile seemed tired. "I am hoping it will keep going until he is better. And speaking of Arturo, there are groceries in the van needing to be carried to the kitchen, and he cannot do it."

Myron dropped the end of the sheet he had been wrestling with. "Sure. We can carry," he said as he nodded in the direction of Adam. The two young men followed Elena out of the laundry room.

The doors at the end of the hall were propped open. A man leaning heavily on a cane was standing beside the open sliding door of a white van. It was stuffed with boxes and bags stacked on the passenger seats and crammed along the floorboards.

At the door, Elena said, "This is my husband, Arturo." They shook hands all around as she made the introductions.

"Now, you go and sit in the recliner," Elena said to Arturo. "You are doing too much, and the doctor said you will not heal if you do not do what he tells you. Myron and Adam can carry this to this kitchen. I will get Soosie to help Alma put the things away." She urged her husband along the hall toward the front of the building.

Each of the young men hefted a box and headed to the kitchen where Alma, who was not much taller than Elena, was clearing the wide island.

"Set it here," she said.

Putting his box down, Myron turned and bumped into Soosie. He reared back and immediately apologized before making a wide berth around the island as he headed back to the van.

Alma grinned at the girl. "What did you do to scare him so bad? He jumped like he expected you to stick a knife in his heart."

Soosie responded with a ghost of a smile.

* * * * *

Just before three thirty, Elena bustled into the laundry room, carrying three bags. Pausing in the doorway, she looked around. "Everything is so nice," she said, nodding approvingly.

"It's Adam," Myron said. "He seems to know a lot about this stuff, although Soosie helped us conquer those fitted sheets."

"Well, I am glad you are now here. Our people keep saying how nice it is to see young faces. It helps them feel good. I am bringing you more uniforms. My sons worked here when they were in high school and college, but now they are grown. For you, Soosie, some of Angie's she wore before the babies."

She handed over the bags and glanced at the clock on the wall. "And now your day is finished. Come, let me show you how to clock out."

Alma stuck her head in the door. "Oh, good, you're still here." She waved three small plastic bags. "Here is a snack to tide you over until you get some dinner. My kids are always starved when they get home from school or work." She passed the bags out. "Speaking of which, I have a middle-schooler who is probably wondering where his ride is. See you tomorrow." She was already digging in her purse for her keys as she headed back out.

At the desk in the main room, Elena had them note their time on a sheet of paper. "Tomorrow, we will get your pictures, and I will order proper identification badges for you to use for the time clock."

Chapter 4

T he adrenalin that had kept the teens pumped all day dissipated on the bus ride home. They tiredly made their way through the front door.

"I'll let them know we're back," Myron said, turning right toward the office while the other two silently headed for the stairs.

In his room, Adam dropped onto his bed. After a moment, he leaned over and fished in the bag Elena had given them to pull out the cookies. As he took a big bite of one, he spotted a pile of sheets, blankets, and a pillow on the other bed in the room.

His shoulders slumped as he recognized he was about to get another roommate. His brain wondered for a moment how many this would make in the two-plus years he had been living at the Pitt, but the thought wilted as soon as it blossomed. It was just one more thing on his ever-lengthening list of things that were too much trouble to care about.

His bed was positioned against the wall with the door, so he couldn't see who opened it. Then a navy-blue duffle bag edged its way into view. It was followed by an arm attached to Myron.

"The room mothers want me to move in here with you since we are both on the same schedule now," Myron said. "Do you mind?"

Adam stuffed the last of the cookie in his mouth and gestured to the other bed. "All yours," he said in a crumb-muffled voice. "I'm gonna go change."

Adam went to his side of the closet. Although he didn't have a lot of clothes, what he did have was thrown haphazardly on top of the small dresser filling the lower part of the closet and jammed on the small shelf above with a few more things slung over the clothes rod. He dug around until he found a pair of sweatpants and a tee-shirt.

It wasn't modesty propelling him to the bathroom. With two twin beds, a small bookcase between the beds, and the closet, space to move around in the room was minimal. Just putting a shirt on meant, sooner or later, the room's other occupant was going to get decked.

* * * * *

Following dinner, Adam watched as Myron meticulously made his bed. It was like something he saw once in some military movie where the guy bounced a quarter off the blanket to make sure it was taut enough.

Then Myron began to put his clothes away, hanging his khaki pants and polo shirts. Since each side of the closet only held about a half-dozen hangers, they were soon full, and he began to refold the remaining items.

"Go ahead and use the ones on my side," Adam said.

Finally, Myron stored his bag neatly under the bed.

"You know, man, you're making me look bad," Adam said.

Myron grinned. "You aren't even in the rankings. You should see my folks' place. They make hoarders look tidy." Then his face sobered. "'Course, I'm pretty sure a lot of it has been cleared out now—taken into evidence as probable stolen goods."

Adam's eyes widened. "Stolen goods?"

"Yeah, my dad is the family fence. They steal, he sells, and the money gets split. He used to help steal until my mom crashed the car drunk driving. Smashed his leg up pretty good. Slowed him down too much."

"Geez, I thought the stories about your family were, you know, bullshit."

Myron shook his head. "No, a lot of it is true; the Tatums don't play nice with the law. I've spent my whole life trying not to be them. Still, it doesn't matter how hard I try to be the white sheep of the family, everyone always assumes I'm automatically guilty of something just because my last name is Tatum."

"Like Soosie."

He nodded dejectedly. "Yeah, like Soosie—and pretty much everybody else in Soda Springs," he added quietly.

★★★★★

Above their heads, Soosie was ensnared in a dream.

He was striding ahead of her, his long legs covering great pieces of real estate while she fell farther and farther behind. She was calling frantically after him, "Dad, wait…please wait."

He stopped once to look back at her. "I can't do it, Dad. I've tried so hard, and I can't do it. Please come home."

His expression was mournful as he shook his head. Then he turned away and disappeared in the crowd of people all hurrying away from her.

Soosie jolted awake, struggling to breathe—just as she had

when she learned her father was dead. She pushed hard against the reality, but it rushed in to engulf her. There was no end to the nightmare. It was real and would last forever. Dreams couldn't bring back her father.

It was like the black hole his absence left in their lives had sucked away every good thought, kind action, or reasonable event. All that remained of the life they once had was a pathetic reality show fueled by her mother's and sister's endless drama and poor decisions. It was like they had used her dad's death as an excuse to drop any semblance of responsibility until everything went so crazy, she just couldn't hold it together by herself anymore.

She wrapped her arms around her pillow, pulling it tight against the gnawing hollow emptiness in her center. She buried her face, and hot tears flowed again. But no matter how much she cried, she could never get to the bottom of her anger and pain, never find the place where she felt safe.

Chapter 5

T he next morning when the kids arrived at the care center, it
felt different. There was no one in sight—not Elena, Olivia,
Lidiya, or any of the residents. The silent air felt somber.

Making their way to the laundry room, they saw all the doors to
the rooms were still closed. The only visible light was in the kitchen.

At the laundry room door, Adam reached inside and flipped
on the light switches then stood back to let Soosie enter first before following.

Squatting just outside to retie his shoelace, Myron felt cool
morning air brush against his bare arms. He looked up as Olivia
quietly opened both back doors while a vehicle pulled in adjacent
to them. Small gold letters in the large side window discreetly
stated Watkins Funeral Home. A tall man in an impeccable suit
the same color as the pearl-gray vehicle stepped out and opened
the back hatch of the vehicle. He pulled out a gurney with a bag
neatly folded in the center and maneuvered it through the open
doors and in the direction of the large back room.

Inside the laundry room, Soosie studied the cleaning chart,
running her finger down the tasks to remind herself of everything
she needed to do. Going to the cleaning cupboard, she pulled
out one of the caddies holding supplies and headed to the door.

Myron was standing squarely in the center of it.

"Move it, Tatum," she said. Her voice bathed his last name in venom.

"I think it might be better if you wait a few minutes," Myron said quietly.

"Don't tell me what to do." She tried to push past him.

He put his hands on her shoulders to stop her forward motion. "Please, don't go now."

She lashed out and slapped him hard across the face. "Don't you touch me. Don't you ever touch me." Flinging her arm up, she muscled her way past him into the hall where the open back doors caught her attention.

The sight of the hearse slammed her in the diaphragm, stopped her breath, and whiplashed her into a time tunnel where she once again heard her mom's phone ringing and ringing and she was running to find it. It lay on the floor next to the couch where her mother had fallen asleep the night before. Grabbing it, she clicked to the call.

"Hello?"

"Mrs. Fretwell, we need you to come to immediately," a coolly efficient voice said.

"Why, what's wrong?" Panic underscored every word.

"Soosie?" the voice asked. "I'm sorry, hon, you sounded like your mom. Would you please tell her we need her to come right now. There has been a change in your dad."

The pill bottles lining the coffee table had more than done their job of putting her mother in a deep place of forgetfulness. It had taken so long to get her mom awake enough to understand the urgency of the call.

When her mother was finally able to stumble into the bathroom, Soosie had run to wake her sister, but the room was empty. Again.

Her mother's reaction had been negligible when Soosie told her. "Well, you know, honey, your sister's had a real rough time with your dad's situation and all."

Those words had dug painfully into Soosie's heart. Her mother was always talking about everything her older sister was going through because of her father's accident but never acknowledging he was also Soosie's father and she was going through the same events.

When she and her mom had finally wheeled into the parking lot at the convalescent home, they passed a tall man closing the back door on the hearse. Through the side window, Soosie had been able to see an indistinct human form encased in a brown bag.

Not even waiting for the car to be shifted into park, she had flown out the door, racing into the building and down the hall to her father's room.

His bed was empty, stripped bare. The top of the nightstand was also bare of its usual items. A small box containing the few personal items they had brought was packed and sitting on the guest chair.

Her heart slammed into her chest wall with each beat shrieking "*No! No! No!*"

It was later when her brain recognized the lumpy bag in the back of the hearse had been her father.

The abrupt heaving of her stomach snapped her back to the present. She spun and sprinted for the employee's bathroom.

She made it just in time.

★★★★★

Adam stared at the angry red mark across Myron's cheek. "Geez, man, are you okay?"

Myron looked away, but Adam caught a sheen of unshed tears in his eyes. They were gone when he looked back.

"What the hell was that all about anyway?" Adam asked.

Myron silently shook his head and crossed to the cleaning cupboard.

* * * * *

In the bathroom, Soosie leaned over the sink rinsing out her mouth with handfuls of water before wiping the cold perspiration from her face with a wet paper towel. As the violent physical reaction subsided, it was replaced with a realization. Myron had seen the hearse and somehow guessed it might upset her. He had actually been trying to shield her.

It was just so wrong. He was a Tatum, and there was no way she would ever accept anything from him, regardless of the motive.

She drew in a several deep breaths to steady herself before cracking open the bathroom door.

Lights were on, and she could hear voices and movement. Chancing a look down the hall, she saw the morning sun glistening on the leaves of the laurel hedge on the other side of the alley and reflecting the light through the windows of the now-closed back doors.

Olivia came out of the back ward pushing the smaller hamper. Behind her, Myron pushed one large hamper and pulled the other.

Olivia waved for her. "Oh good, there you are, Soosie," she said as she maneuvered her hamper into the laundry room.

Soosie knew it would be the appropriate action to take one of the hampers Myron was wrangling. But before she could decide whether or not to snub the thought, Adam stepped out and grabbed the hamper Myron was pushing. But instead of wheeling it into the room, he pulled it past the door to deliberately block her until Myron was inside.

Once Adam had pushed through the door, Soosie used the few moments of the hampers being jostled around to slip in. There was an odd mixture of embarrassment and enmity sloshing in her center.

Chapter 6

With the hampers out of the way, Olivia closed the door. When she turned back, she saw three young faces looking at her in various states of consternation.

"Oh, don't look so scared, y'all. You haven't done a thing wrong. I just want to let you know what's going on.

"First of all, we had a loss today. Miss Meryl in the back ward passed this morning. While I'm right sorry this happened on only your second day here, it was a real blessing she was finally able to fly out of her body that had failed her so long ago. I'm just hoping she is dancin' her ass off on those streets of gold right now.

"Now, since pretty much everybody living here at the center has nobody left to sit with them when they are fixin' to pass, Elena is the one who holds their hands and does the prayin' 'til the angel of death comes to fetch them home.

"She sat with Miss Meryl since about two this morning. Lidiya and I have made her go home to get some shuteye. But it leaves us short-handed for today, so we may need to call on you kids to give a helping hand, if'n you're willing."

As they all nodded their heads, there was a knock on the door. David was on the other side when Olivia opened it.

"Just wanted you to know there has been a witch sighting this morning. Emily spotted the hag sitting in a blue Altima. Still using her camera and scribbling notes."

"Hell's fire, doesn't that woman have anything else to do besides circle this place on her broom? I'm glad Elena went home to sleep; it would upset her something fierce, as if enough trouble hasn't been landing in her lap lately." Olivia stormed out of the room.

David rolled deeper into the room. "I suppose Olivia told you kids about Meryl."

"Yes, sir, she did," Adam said.

"Meryl was one fine lady. A fine lady who got dealt a really crappy hand in this life." David said. "Brilliant educator. She knew how to help kids dream and dream big. You would be amazed how many of those kids succeeded. Then she was diagnosed with progressive multiple sclerosis." He shook his head slowly at the memory.

"She eventually lost her ability to do much of anything. Her husband couldn't handle it and bailed, leaving her dependent on caregivers. The last one just quit showing up. She was left sitting in her wheelchair for two days until one of her neighbors realized he hadn't seen anyone come or go at their place and went to check on her.

"Long story short, even though the whole town proclaimed their love and admiration for Meryl, the only place locally who would take her in was here. She wasn't drawing enough money to cover the costs of the other places. Actually not here either, but Elena just wrote the difference off.

"Then last fall, one of Meryl's students, who has become a pretty well-known artist, donated a sculpture to the grade school honoring Meryl's contribution to the lives of the students who had been privileged to receive her attention. Although they had wanted Meryl to attend, she was no longer physically able.

"So the newspaper asked to interview her. Elena declined it, citing Meryl's deteriorating condition. But old 'take no hostages' Adah shows up a couple of times anyway demanding to talk to Meryl. Elena sent her away with a flea in her ear both times. But damn if she didn't manage to find a time to sneak in while everyone was occupied.

"Might have gotten away with it too, except Tilly saw what was going on and hollered loud and clear. Tilly's body may be twisted up, but her mind is still sharp. When Elena realized Adah had gotten in, she called the police. Bill Hixson showed up and yanked her ass out of here. He was threatening to charge her with trespassing and harassing an incapacitated person while Adah was hollering she was gonna expose this place as a 'death trap.'"

"Is that Adah Skelton, sir?" Myron asked.

"Yup, the wicked witch of the west herself. You know her?"

"Well, kinda. She was on a mission a couple of years back to rid Soda Springs of the Tatum infestation. So she started stalking various family members."

"What happened?"

Myron shrugged. "They stalked back."

"Well, Elena was able to get an injunction against Adah ever coming on or into this place without prior written permission from her or Arturo. The whole dustup led to Adah being dismissed from the paper. She had ridden the connection of her daddy owning the paper for years because it made her feel like she was still a force to be reckoned with in this town. The firing turned her into just another old 'used to be somebody has-been.' Consequently, Adah is fully committed to trying to prove she still has the power by getting this place closed down.

"You kids watch yourselves. When Adah is out to do mayhem, she doesn't care who gets messed up as collateral damage."

Olivia reappeared in the door. "I need some help transferring Clarence to his chair."

Myron stepped forward. "I'll help."

Olivia grinned. "Thanks, but I think it would do Clarence more good if Soosie helped me. Not that you're shabby lookin' or anything, but he much prefers the ladies." She stopped and peered more closely at Myron. The angry red mark was now morphing into an equally angry bruise.

"Boy, what happened to you?" she asked as she pointed to her own cheek.

Myron looked away, catching Adam's eye.

"I punched him...on accident this morning," Adam said. "Our room at the Pitt is pretty small, and Myron stood up just as I was pulling on my scrub top."

"Want me to get some ice to put on it?" Olivia asked.

Myron shook his head. "I'm good. Thank you."

Across the room, Soosie stared at them. They were covering her ass. Why?

"Okay, if you're sure. Come on, Soosie. Clarence is nothing but skin and bones, so he's an easy move. And you, mister, best be getting on up to the breakfast table or Bert's gonna have eaten your breakfast as well."

David backed his wheelchair out of the room. "If it's burnt gruel again, she's welcome to it."

With the exception of times when Olivia or Lidiya fetched one or another of them to help, the three teens went about their duties silently. Adam and Myron carefully avoided making eye contact with Soosie and did their best to keep their backs to her as much as possible.

As the day progressed, Soosie was more and more bugged about the morning events. Were they expecting some kind of payoff for not ratting her out? Were they waiting until they could talk to the night counselor, Jarett? Were they setting her up for a big fat fall?

Each passing hour found the questions consuming a larger and larger portion of her thoughts as she tried to figure all possible angles.

Finally, Alma distributed carefully wrapped brownies to each of them, and the day was over.

*****

Instead of offering to report their homecoming to the room mothers, Myron just climbed up to their room with Adam right behind him. Once in the room, Myron sprawled on his bed, putting his arm across his eyes.

Sitting on his own bed, Adam watched him. "So, are you going tell me what exactly happened today, or am I going wonder the rest of my life why the hell I helped save Soosie Fretwell's butt when she'd just as soon push ours under a bus after cutting out our hearts with a rattail comb?"

"Maybe because you're a good guy?" Myron said without uncovering his eyes.

"'Good guy' is totally not in my intake description. Do better."

Myron lowered his arm. "So remember when the room mothers told us about working at the care center? As soon as they announced it, Soosie got upset."

Adam shook his head. "Since she tried to push a pointed object through my chest earlier, I was pretty focused on ignoring her."

"There is that. But when she looked like she was going pass out yesterday right as we first arrived, I wondered if the care center was a good gig for her, so I mentioned it to Jarett yesterday. He told me Soosie's father had died in a nursing home after sustaining an irreversible head injury."

"And that explains today's random act of violence how?"

"The hearse for Meryl pulled up at the back door right after you guys had gone into the laundry room. I thought it might upset Soosie to see it."

A buzzer sounded. Adam stood up, but Myron gave no sign of planning to move.

"You coming to dinner?"

Myron just shook his head and fixed his eyes on the ceiling. Adam pushed his brownie to Myron's side of the bookcase. "Here," he said and left the room.

✶✶✶✶✶

The kids were just finishing dinner when Jarett came into the dining area. Looking around the table, he pointed to an empty chair. "Where's Myron?"

"Headache," Adam said as he gathered up his plate and silverware to take to the kitchen.

"Well, tell him to come down, and I'll give him a couple of

44

aspirins. And come back with him. Soosie, you as well. I need to see the three of you in my office. Now."

Soosie shot a look at Adam, but he turned away before she could read his face. Was this the moment they were going to drop the hammer on her?

Chapter 7

J arett pointed when they entered. "Dudes, you two take the couch, Soosie can have the chair. How's the headache, Myron? You need some aspirin?"

"No. Thank you. It's better."

Jarett leaned in to peer at the bruise on Myron's face. "What the hell happened to your face?"

Myron pasted on a wry smile. "Always close the upper cabinet doors before bending over to put things in the lower cabinet."

Jarett nodded. "Sounds like a good safety tip. Now, I want to read you something from today's Soda Springs *Sentinel*."

He proceeded to read them a diatribe in the form of a letter to the editor against the Soda Springs Care Center. It itemized faults with the physical plant, including the unfinished painting of the front of the building and the unkempt state of the flowerbeds. It suggested the front steps and the wheelchair ramp were possibly unsafe as well. Then, after insinuating the state of the interior was possibly as bad or worse than the exterior, it ended by questioning the safety of the residents in an apparently deteriorating physical plant.

"So, I know today was only your second day, but you kids aren't dummies. Is anything going on that makes you uncomfortable or might indicate it's a shoddy operation? Basically, are you

47

seeing or experiencing anything you think would be a reason I should pull you out?"

The surprise in the faces of all three teens answered his question.

"I know we're new there, but it feels like a good place. Elena, er, Mrs. Fuentes, looks after everybody like they're her family." Myron looked at Adam and Soosie, "Even us." Soosie and Adam nodded their agreement.

Jarett tossed the paper back on his desk. "Okay. I just wanted to be sure. I don't know what this is all about, but if you feel like anything is going south, I want to know immediately. None of you are far from aging out of this place, and all your records are pretty good right now, so we want to do our part in keeping it that way."

He waved at the door. "Myron, go fix yourself a sandwich since you missed dinner. We're done."

✳ ✳ ✳ ✳ ✳

Myron was just finishing washing down a second peanut butter and jelly sandwich with the last of the milk he had brought up from the kitchen when there was a sharp knock on the door frame and Soosie's face peered in at them through their open door.

"I want to find out what's going on," she said bluntly.

Since house rules strictly forbade members of opposite sexes from being in bedrooms at the same time, she stood squarely in the doorway, feet apart and arms crossed over her chest.

Adam leaned out of his bed to peer around the open door before disappearing from Soosie's line of vision.

"Three times today you could have fried my ass but didn't. Why?"

"Maybe because you don't need more bad stuff in your life," Myron said.

"What the hell do you know about my life? What the hell do you Tatums know about 'bad stuff'?"

Adam vaulted into view. "Are you a complete bimbo brain? Did it ever occur to you you're not the only one sentenced to the Pitt because of a totally screwed family? Did you get to pick your family before shooting out into this world? Well, neither did Myron or me. So you've had some shitty breaks? Man, so have we. I saved your ass because of Myron. He's the only one of us who doesn't spend all his time wallowing in a mosh pit of pity. He actually freakin' cares enough to notice other people have issues and problems too.

"Yeah, you're damned right he could have fried you, and instead of being grateful that you aren't heading back to juvie or wherever right this sec, you're here trash-talking him. You keep blatting on about the no-good, rotten Tatums. Myron's got the concept, but there is nothing he can do about it. He's been paying his whole life for other people's shit, and now you wanna collect too. Here's a news flash: he didn't owe it to you this morning when he tried to keep you from seeing something he thought would be upsetting, and he sure as hell don't owe you now." Adam swung the door shut.

Chapter 8

Dropping back on his bed, Adam looked over at Myron. The expression on Myron's face could only be described as dumbfounded. "What?"

"You just stood up for me. The only other person who has ever done that is Chief Braden."

"Chief Braden? Really? That's funny because he probably saved my life when I was a little kid," Adam said. "Iris and Velma sure didn't give a shit."

"Iris and Velma? Who are they?"

"My mom and grandmother, but they just weren't into the whole 'kid thing,' so they liked to pretend I was just some stray they were keeping an eye on. It was more believable if I used their names."

Myron settled his pillow in the corner of the bed. "So what happened?"

"When I began first grade, they decided I could take care of myself. We lived in an apartment just a couple of blocks from the school, so I walked both ways. Sometimes they came home after they closed the beauty shop for the day, and sometimes not. I pretty much fended for myself—watching TV and eating whatever I could find, which wasn't much at all some of the time.

"So this one day I took a header off the swing at school and broke my arm." Adam unconsciously rubbed his left arm. "The school made a splint out of folded cardboard and taped my arm to it. They called my mom. She came and got me, but she just took me home because she had appointments waiting at the shop and then plans with Velma to go out.

"The next morning was their late morning to open at the shop, so they were both still sleeping when it was time for me to go to school. They didn't like it when I had to stay home sick, so I took myself off. I was crying when I got to the school because I hadn't slept much and because my arm hurt so bad. My teacher hauled me down to the office.

"I cried harder when Chief Braden showed up. I was sure I was in major trouble. That Iris and Velma had sent him to arrest me. They were always threatening to have me arrested and locked up in some place where you got beat every day for being a bad boy."

"That's messed up," Myron said.

"Anyway, the chief loaded me in his patrol car, which would have been totally cool if I hadn't been so scared, and went to the apartment. He pounded on the door until Velma answered. I don't know what he said to her, because he came back and drove me to the hospital. He stayed with me while they were x-raying my arm and setting it. The whole time the doctor was asking me lots of questions about what I ate, what I did after school, who babysat me, and other stuff.

"I don't really know what went down between the chief and my mom when she showed up at the hospital, but afterwards she picked me up every day at the school office and took me back to the shop until I really was old enough to fend for myself."

"There wasn't anyone else in your family who could have looked out for you?"

"Not that I ever knew about."

"And you really don't know who your dad is?"

Adam's lips compressed into a thin line. "Not a clue."

* * * * *

Upstairs, Soosie lay on her bed watching the light fade from the sky. There were some hard thoughts banging around in her head. She had felt so totally justified in burning Myron with her anger because his last name was Tatum. Now Adam's words were calling her out.

She had been making Myron pay for what another Tatum had done. And, yeah, she knew it was wrong. It was just that Myron was here, and the guilty one was out of reach for the time being.

A harsh question formed. Jerking Myron around was going to accomplish what? Did she really believe the justice she wanted to render so desperately was going to happen through Myron? That somehow by punishing him, retribution, like some weird virus, would be transmitted through all the Tatums?

Some of the heat burning in her core dampened a little. Okay, she bargained with herself. She would lighten up on Myron—for now. But if he stepped over any boundary she set, all bets were off, and he would once again be fair game. He had earned her distance, but that was it.

Chapter 9

The next morning, instead of climbing the stairs to the care center, Myron wandered down the sidewalk staring at the building. A fresh, buttery cream-colored paint covered about one third of the building before dribbling off into a dirty pale grey. Grass crept up through the bark dust, and the little boxwoods scattered along the front needed a good trim.

With one foot on the bottom step, Adam paused to watch him while Soosie, realizing she had reached the door without either of the males, turned back.

"Forget where we work?" Adam asked.

"Nah. Just looking," Myron answered absently as he joined Adam and they followed Soosie into the building.

Heading to the laundry, they saw Paul, who was wearing green pedal pushers and a peasant top embroidered in matching green, standing in the doorway of his room peering down the hall in their direction. As soon as he saw them, he hollered, "Soooosie!"

"I'm pretty sure I know whose day it is for personal laundry," Adam said. He flipped on the lights and quickly checked the chart.

"Yup," he said. "Paul it is."

Bustling by, Olivia shot a quick grin to Soosie. "Best be answering, sweetie. Paulie will hound a body to death until he gets what he's trackin' on."

Gathering their cleaning caddies, the young men headed out. Soosie wore a sour expression as she pushed Paul's laundry hamper back to the laundry room before gathering her own cleaning caddy.

"I got a detailed lecture from Paul this morning on exactly how he wants his 'dainties' washed, so I guess I'm going to have to handwash everything pretty much, except for his shorts, pajamas, and socks. He said those can go through the washing machine." She gave an exasperated sigh as she pushed the hamper to the small sink.

"Use the basket," Adam said, pointing to the shelf over the smaller washing machine.

Myron circled around the folding table and lifted a small green basket down.

Unsmilingly, Soosie snatched it out of his hands.

Myron silently returned to the soaking sink.

Adam came over to where Soosie stood, opened the washing machine, and showed her how to put it over the agitator. "Put the clothes in, then just use the delicate cycle—"

A loud thunk interrupted his instructions, and the gurgle of water being pumped out of the large washing machine stopped.

"That doesn't sound good," Myron said mildly.

Adam leapt back across the room and quickly shut the machine off. "The drain pump just crapped out," he said. "And this machine's out of business until it's replaced."

"Want me to get Elena?" Myron said.

Adam shook his head. "Hang on a minute." He crossed to a cupboard in the opposite corner and opened it. Inside were the usual miscellany for maintenance and repairs. He pulled out an open box and poked inside. "If the part is here, I've got this. And this is the part, I do believe."

He reached back in to drag a tool box off the bottom shelf. Sitting both items on the folding table, he flipped open the tool box and rummaged around. "Yeah, we're good."

Myron looked uncertain. "You sure?"

"I told you I was raised in a strip mall. Mr. Orenco at the Suds 'n' Duds let me hang out and help him for years. He was letting me change out pumps by the time I got to middle school. Myron, can you give me a hand pulling this out so I can unplug it?"

After wrestling the washing machine away from the wall, Adam unplugged it from the outlet. Securing a flathead screwdriver from the tool box, he opened the control panel and disconnected a wire. Then with Myron's help, they removed the machine cover.

Grabbing a wrench and the new drain pump, Adam dropped to the floor and quickly replaced the old pump. Another ten minutes of putting it back together and Adam was able to plug it in. The two teens wrangled it back into position. Adam pulled the knob, reengaging the cycle. The water began to drain steadily.

"Things should speed up now," he said, putting the tools away.

Soosie stared at him. It was the second time Adam had totally surprised her, first by his hard push-back speech of last night and now his skill set. It occurred to her the "dumb-ass," as she always thought of him, might have something resembling a brain after all. The realization was vaguely unsettling.

* * * * *

At the end of the day, they took their usual places on the transit bus. Soosie sat in the front seat, while Myron and Adam sat back several rows. She could hear an occasional buzz of words between them, but their voices were too quiet for her to actually hear what they were saying.

She fingered the homemade granola in the baggie Alma had given them for their ride home. Something was nibbling at the edge of her thoughts but so far defied identification. The protocol she established on day one meant she walked ahead when they trekked the last two blocks back to the Pitt and then beelined for her room. Today was no different. Once she had changed into her jeans and tee-shirt, she sat on her bed, waiting for the dinner buzzer.

Across the hall, she could hear the other two girls living at the Pitt. They were younger than she was. Alesha was fourteen and Chelsea was fifteen. Both were temps, meaning their stay was limited to waiting for some circumstance to occur that would secure their release.

Although they had latched on to each other and left Soosie alone when they were assigned to the same room, this week they had suddenly begun to pull the whole BFF thing with her. It had taken all of two nanoseconds to realize they were nursing crushes on Myron and Adam and were trying to pump her for information. She shut them down pretty hard.

"Guess somebody is keeping all the goodies for herself," Chelsea had snarked as they headed back to the room, slamming the door for good measure. Since then, they had been playing freeze-out, as if she cared.

She looked around and, for the billionth time since she got here, wished she had books to read. They had always been the friends she could count on to be there when she needed them. There certainly weren't any others left in her life.

At dinner, she glanced at Myron and Adam. They sat side-by-side, eating with their heads down. Surreptitiously watching them, she realized they never actually made eye contact with anyone at the table, just quietly packed the food away.

Both of them had just picked up their plates and utensils when Jarett passed through the room.

"You wanted to talk to me, Myron?" he said.

"Yes, sir."

Adam reached out and took Myron's plate. "I got this," he said as he headed to the kitchen. Myron followed Jarett in the direction of the office.

Soosie took care of her dishes and then climbed up to her room. Sitting on her bed, she realized Adam and Myron were apparently becoming friends. And inexplicably, a splinter of jealousy shot through her.

Chapter 10

The next morning Soosie scooted out of the laundry room. She liked to vacuum Emily's room while she was out for her morning walk. It gave Soosie a chance to sneak a few minutes to read over the various book titles in Emily's burgeoning bookcases.

She swiftly vacuumed the room before perusing the shelves. Having carefully looked over the titles on the upper shelves, she squatted down to read book titles along the lower shelves.

"Do I see another bibliophile?"

Soosie flushed and jumped up. "I'm sorry. I shouldn't—"

Although spring had arrived, the weather was still cool first thing in the morning, and Emily was dressed to match it. The tall, older woman wore blue jeans and a baja hoodie over a long-sleeved gray Henley tee-shirt. Red socks peeked out of her Birkenstock sandals. Her iron-gray hair hung down her back in a long braid.

Emily waved her dismissal as she shrugged off the hoodie. "Oh, my dear. I can assure you I would have definitely done the same thing. To some of us, books call the way the sirens called to Odysseus. What do you like to read?"

"Fantasy and science fiction mostly. Some mysteries."

"Do you have books at the Pittison House?"

Soosie shook her head. "Not many. Mainly what somebody left when they moved out."

"And let me guess. You have read everything you could find."

"Even a couple of romances, which I hate."

"I will warn you my actual collection, while well curated, is mainly older classics in the various genres. However, I would be delighted to select several and loan them to you. When you have finished them, bring them back and we'll choose others. And if you would like, we can discuss them during your lunch hour. Although I retired long ago from teaching college lit, I still can't resist talking about books. David and I have some really splendid debates."

Soosie's face beamed. "That would be so wonderful. Thank you. Thank you."

"Stop by after lunch, and I will have them ready for you."

* * * * *

As soon as lunch was over, Soosie headed to Emily's room. The older woman had several books stacked on her small desk.

"I've chosen the first two books from a classic fantasy series and two classic science fiction," Emily said. "Ursula LeGuin's *The Wizard of Earthsea* and *The Tombs of Autuan* are marvelous fantasy. For science fiction, I have selected two works considered seminal. Robert Heinlein's *Stranger in a Strange Land* and a book that has become very apropos today, Ray Bradbury's *Fahrenheit 451*." She paused and looked at Soosie. "You haven't read them already, have you? If you have, we can choose others."

Soosie shook her head.

"I thought not. These were published well before your time." Emily looked past Soosie as she reflected. "Actually, they were probably originally published before your parents' time." She looked back at Soosie with a wistful smile. "Sometimes I forget just how very old I am."

Emily slipped the books into a tote bag and handed them over. "I'm looking forward to seeing what you think of them."

Soosie hugged the bag to her chest. "Thank you."

★ ★ ★ ★ ★

The folding table in the laundry room was full of towels when Soosie slipped in. She carefully sat the bag on the chair next to the maintenance cupboard.

Elena bustled into the room. "I just want to come thank you for helping Olivia and Lidiya yesterday. We do not have many staff, so it is difficult sometimes when someone is not present."

The washing machine behind Adam smoothly shifted gears, and the water could be heard draining steadily.

Elena cocked her head as she listened. "The machine sounds like it is working as it should."

"The old pump conked out yesterday," Adam said. "Luckily the new part Mr. Fuentes had ordered was in the cupboard, so we were able to fix it." He motioned to include Myron.

Myron held up his hands. "Adam fixed it, not me. I just provided some muscle."

Adam went rigid when Elena rushed to him and threw her arms around him. Elena stepped back. "I think you have not had many hugs in your life, but no matter. Here you must put up with them and maybe find they are not so bad to get."

Myron cleared his throat. "Ummm, Elena. We saw the letter in the paper yesterday."

Elena immediately bristled. "That woman. She lives just to make trouble. Arturo was painting the wall when he had his accident. The ladder shifted and he fell. Now he cannot finish it until he is better. It does not look good, but there is nothing we can do about it. It is very expensive to hire a painter to finish it. The money I have must take care of my people first. They cannot eat a wall or take it as their medicine." She pivoted and left the room.

As soon as she was out of sight, Myron and Adam exchanged looks. Something passed between them that Soosie could not translate.

Chapter 11

Although she carefully arranged them in the little bookcase in her room, Soosie refrained from actually beginning to read any of the books until after supper.

Back in her room, she propped herself up and reached for *Fahrenheit 451*. She gently ran her hand over the cover and breathed a sigh of contentment. Tonight, she would not be lonely.

＊＊＊＊＊

The next afternoon, Soosie watched suspiciously as David rolled in and told the two boys Elena wanted to see them in her office. Both of them were nonchalant, as though they had been expecting the summons. It was some minutes before they came back. Neither said anything to her or each other as they picked up where they had left off on their laundry tasks.

As Soosie folded David's sweats, irritation began to buzz in her. The guys seemed to think they didn't have to acknowledge her or let her know what was happening. It was like they belonged to some kind of secret club marked "No Girls Allowed."

Despite the rational part of her brain pointing out she herself had posted the first sign stating an unequivocal warning, "Danger—Do Not Approach," the thought did not abate her irritation.

Myron and Adam were carefully observing the boundaries she had set, and it was totally pissing her off. And why was she feeling this way when she hated Myron and thought Adam was Soda Springs's biggest loser?

The fact that nothing surging inside of her was making any kind of sense made her want to grab her hair and scream.

She glanced at the clock to gauge how long it would be until she could run to her hole at the Pitt and bury herself in the books Emily loaned her. Tomorrow was Friday, and she would have the whole weekend to live someone else's life. She hoped the fictional lives waiting to be read would make more sense than her own.

After dinner, she was headed back upstairs for her literary meetup with Guy Montag and Clarisse McClellan when Jarett's voice stopped her.

"So what time are you planning on heading out Saturday?" he was asking someone.

Turning, she saw he was addressing Myron while Adam was poised a couple of steps up from him.

"Since it is the weekend, the first bus doesn't go until 8:00 a.m. Mr. Fuentes is meeting us at 8:30 with all the stuff."

"Fine. If you aren't done by the last bus, call. We'll come pick you up."

*****

Sitting on her bed, Soosie stared with unseeing eyes at the book waiting for her on the bookcase while she tried to figure out what Myron and Adam were up to.

On their first day, Elena had explained the graveyard shift people would do whatever laundry might be necessary on the weekend; otherwise, it just piled up until they showed up on Monday, so she could rule that out. Plus, they were meeting with Mr. Fuentes, not Elena. And whatever they were up to obviously had the room mothers' approval.

Damn their secretive hides. Okay, no friggin' problem. She would be sure to be up and waiting as well. "See you at eight on Saturday, boys," she said and picked up her book.

*****

"Dude, you do not wear khakis and a polo shirt to do grubby work," Adam said as he watched Myron pull clothes out of his side of the closet. "Wear something you don't care if it gets wrecked."

Myron stood holding his pants and shirt. "This is pretty much all I have."

Adam rummaged around in his closet and tossed Myron a pair of torn jeans and a trashed sweatshirt.

The two raggedy teens trotted down the stairs to find Soosie waiting by the front door.

"What are you up to?" she asked bluntly.

"We're going to finish painting the front of the care center," Adam said.

Soosie shrugged. "Then I'm going too."

Myron and Adam exchanged looks.

"Don't give me that boys' club shit," she snapped. "I work there as well as you, and you can't keep me from going with you."

Adam sighed, "Whatever."

Chapter 12

A battered pickup truck was parked in front of the center when the kids got off the bus. The back end was filled with ladders, paint cans, drop cloths, brushes, rollers, trays, and some safety cones.

Adam dropped the tailgate and picked up a couple of cones. He thrust them at Soosie. "Here, block off the sidewalk."

He and Myron pulled out the ladders and leaned them against the building. "I'll brush along the eaves and around the windows if you want to roll the walls to start," Myron said. "We can trade off after a while."

"Sounds good."

"And I'm to do what?" Soosie asked.

Before either boy could answer, Elena bustled up, beaming. "Myron, Adam. How happy this makes me. And Soosie? You came as well."

"Yeah," Soosie stammered. "I thought maybe you could use some extra help."

Elena immediately pointed down. "The flowerbeds are very sad. Maybe you would not mind to make them happy again? Then everything will be nice. There are some gloves and clippers in the cupboard in the laundry room."

Once Myron and Adam had everything they needed to paint and Soosie was sitting on the sidewalk tugging grass and dandelions out of the flower bed, Elena headed out with the pickup to locate bark dust to freshen the beds.

As soon as the truck disappeared around the corner, a blue Altima edged into sight. A heavyset woman in orthopedic shoes got out. Standing next to the car, she held up her cell phone and began shooting pictures of the kids.

*****

Soosie was sweeping the last of the stray bark dust into the flowerbeds while Adam and Myron were loading the ladders and other painting equipment back into the truck when David called from the porch.

"Need to borrow one of you guys for a minute," he said gesturing to the door.

Adam was still maneuvering his ladder into the truck, so Myron headed to the porch.

Inside, Elena waited with a tall, nicely dressed woman. "Myron, this is Mary. She has just returned. Mary, this is Myron. He is one of three young people who have come to help us while Angie is out with the baby and Arturo with his back. I do not think he would mind about bringing in your suitcases."

Myron shook his head. "Not at all. Just let me wash my hands."

Adam and Soosie came in as well after they'd finished loading everything in the truck.

Adam stopped short when the woman standing with Elena was obviously startled as she looked at him. "Joe?" She took a step closer, still studying his face. "Joe?" she asked again softly.

"Mary, this is Adam. He is another of the young people. And this is Soosie," Elena said.

Myron passed behind them with the suitcases and carried them into the room marked with Mary's name. He set them down next to a small corner curio cabinet. Straightening up, he found himself looking at a picture of a face nearly identical to the face he saw on the other side of his room at the Pitt every day.

He peered closer. The portrait was obviously decades old, but the face looking out of it was Adam. An odd vibration crawled down his spine.

Before he could leave her room, Mary hurried in. She tossed her sweater and purse on the bed before grabbing the picture he had just been studying and hurrying back out the door. Myron followed her as she scurried up the hall, holding the photo tight against her chest.

"I'm sorry, I thought you were someone else, but this might explain," Mary said as she held up the picture for Adam to see.

The color drained from Adam's face. "Who is that?" he asked in hoarse whisper.

Mary turned the picture back to herself and gently ran her fingertips over the glass. "It was my son, Joe. He died in 1999." She looked back at Adam. "You look enough like him to be his son."

Adam looked like he had been sucker-punched. Soosie and Myron exchanged glances.

Elena, too, had noticed the effect of Mary's revelation on Adam. She offered a graceful exit. "You all have worked so hard today. We should get you home," she said. "Arturo has the van, so you can all fit."

Chapter 13

Once they were back at the Pitt, Myron herded Adam in the direction of their room. Adam dropped down on the edge of his bed, his hands hanging limply from forearms balanced on his thighs. He simply stared into space.

Myron collected clean clothes from his closet and quietly went to take a shower. Adam had not moved when he returned. Sitting down on his own bed, Myron silently watched.

Finally Adam let out a kind of anguished growl and scraped his fingers through his thick blonde hair. "It's just crazy," he said. "Freakin' creepy crazy!"

"Is there any chance?" Myron asked. "Could your mom have…?"

Adam jumped to his feet and began to pace the few steps it took to cover the distance between the bookcase and the closet and back.

"No way. My dad was just a sperm donor."

"You mean like they got it on one time and she never saw him again?"

"No, I mean like I came out of a Petri dish. Iris had artificial insemination."

"But you said she wasn't into the kid thing, so why would she—"

"Because of her partner."

Myron was looking thoroughly perplexed.

Adam clarified. "Iris is a lezzie. She met this chick when she was going to beauty school. They were together for several years when the chick decided they needed a baby. I'm pretty sure Iris wasn't into the idea, but she wanted her partner happy, so I happened."

"So if this chick wanted you and your mom didn't, why'd your mom keep you?"

"Revenge. She didn't want me, but I was payback for whatever went down between them when it all went bust. Velma told me I was the biggest mistake of Iris's life." He stopped and drew a deep breath. "I'm gonna go take a shower, man. Sorry for freaking."

Adam rummaged through his closet and then disappeared out the door.

*****

Long after they had turned out the lights and Myron's breathing had settled in rhythmic slumber, Adam lay staring at the ceiling.

Once he had been old enough to understand there were such things as dads, he had begun to wonder if he had a dad. He knew from hearing other kids that he wasn't the only one who didn't have a dad living with them, but most of them seemed to at least know who their dad was.

When he finally asked about who fathered him, Iris had blown it off with the whole sperm donor statement. Since he hadn't figured out the birds-and-bees thing, it just confused him. By the time he had reached junior high, he had found out *sperm donor* usually referred to some dude who had gotten it on with a mom and then vanished in the morning, never to be seen or heard from again.

The idea had been a little hard to visualize, since he had never seen his mom actually go out with a man, but it also ignited a tiny flame of hope that maybe somewhere in this big world there was someone who had fathered him, and maybe they would eventually meet.

Then came the night he was jettisoned.

Apparently Iris and her latest squeeze were planning on taking things to the next level, which meant they were moving in together. He had come home from school to find his stuff in a duffle bag and backpack waiting by the door. Velma took his cell phone and his apartment key, and boom—he was on the streets.

He had walked across town in the rain, heading to Suds 'n' Duds. It was warm, dry, and open. He had some change in his pocket, so he could get a snack out of the vending machine to hold him while he tried to figure out what to do.

Once there, he had opened his backpack looking for a dry sweatshirt, and found a large manila envelope. Inside had been his birth certificate, immunization records, along with a white envelope containing papers from a fertility clinic. Sitting in a plastic chair across from a row of silent washing machines, it finally fell together. When Iris had said sperm donor, she had meant it literally.

He still remembered the coldness coursing through his body when the hope there might be someone else in the world for him flamed out. It left a deep, hollow place which had informed his life since then.

Then today he was shown a face which might be his own belonging to a dead man. The tight little construct he had established when he was fifteen and sitting alone in a laundromat was blown. His emotions slammed around like an overloaded washer.

The next morning, he operated by rote. His face was cool and distant as if a part of him had shut down. Respecting his space, Myron still watched protectively.

At the breakfast table, Soosie also covertly watched Adam. And there was concern in her eyes.

Noting it, Myron felt a pang. The only looks he had ever gotten from her were either ice-cold or burning with loathing.

Chapter 14

On Monday morning, Adam paused just outside the door to the center. He drew a deep breath and squared his shoulders before following Soosie inside. He headed to the laundry room without looking right or left.

At lunch, the three kids normally sat at a small table usually reserved for employees. Today as Adam set his tray down, Mary picked up hers from the main table and joined him.

"May I eat with you?" she asked Adam.

His expression was neutral, but he dipped his head slightly.

Myron paused as Mary set her tray down where he usually sat. He didn't think Mary wanted a third party at the table, so he set his own tray down beside Bert at the big table.

When Soosie arrived, David patted the empty chair beside him. "It's safe," he said. "I haven't bitten a young person since I retired from teaching."

"He's moved on to old farts now," Paul growled from his other side.

At the small table situated near the larger ones, Mary folded her hands in her lap. "I want to apologize for Saturday," she said. "I behaved inexcusably by thrusting Joe in your face, but when you walked in looking so much like him, I just reacted without much thought."

Adam kept his eyes focused on the patch of table visible between the two trays.

"See, I had just come home from Corvallis, where I had buried my only sister a few days earlier. She was the last family I had. Everyone else is gone." She looked down at her hands and then back. "Joe never married. He preferred to 'play the field,' to use an old-school phrase. Once I lost him, I sometimes liked to think that maybe in his ramblings he had left a child somewhere, and through some strange coincidence, we would manage to find each other."

Adam finally looked at her. Her smile was diffident. "The silly fantasies of an old woman, and I am wasting too much of your lunch time. Please eat." She picked up her fork, and Adam followed suit.

★ ★ ★ ★ ★

Myron ate while surreptitiously paying attention to what was happening at the small table. Next to him, Bert was noisily digging her spoon into the now-empty strawberry shortcake dish. From the end of the table, Soosie looked over at her with annoyance just in time to see Myron slip his dessert onto her tray. Bert made a gleeful sound and handed her empty dish to him.

David had also observed the exchange. "He's a good man," he said softly to no one in particular.

"He's a Tatum," Soosie snapped.

"Don't see how that's his fault," David countered.

"Our Bert sure loves her food," Steve said as he spooned another mouthful into Clarence. He then forked up some more pasta salad while Clarence gummed and swallowed his lunch mash-up.

When Clarence turned his head to indicate he was ready for another bite, Myron noticed a depression in his skull overlaid with puckered scar tissue. His curiosity as to the cause of the old injury was waylaid when Adam suddenly got up from his table.

Picking up his tray, Adam murmured an "excuse me" and headed toward the hall. Mary watched until he disappeared from view.

Myron could see that Mary's eyes reflected a mix of emotions: hope, fear, joy, and pain. Myron was still watching her when she lowered her eyes and looked right into his.

"You're his friend, aren't you?"

Myron gave a self-deprecating smile. "We share a room at the Pitt, er, Pittison House."

"Pittison House? You don't live with your families?"

"Sometimes things don't work out."

"So Adam doesn't have a family?"

"Actually, he does, kinda."

"Kinda?" Mary repeated.

"It's complicated," Myron sighed as he picked up his tray. "Really complicated."

★ ★ ★ ★ ★

"You know you can do a DNA test," Myron said suddenly from his side of their shared room.

Adam turned his head to look at him. "What are you talking about?"

Myron swung his feet to the floor and sat up. "You know, to see if maybe you are related to Mary. Maybe Joe was a sperm donor."

Adam turned his head back to stare at the ceiling. "Yeah, I'm going to walk in and say, 'Do you mind sticking this swab in your mouth? I wanna find out if I'm your grandson.'"

"Why not?"

Adam propped himself up on his elbow. "Because it's crazy thinking. You're trying to say of all the possible donors, Iris picked the one whose mom is living in a care center where the 'biggest mistake of her life' just happens to get employed." He plopped back down on the bed. "That is pretty freakin' far out."

"Dude, maybe you can get out of yourself long enough to try processing what Mary said to you at lunch today. "

"You heard?"

"Duh. I was, like, about two feet away."

"Yeah? So what did you hear that you think I didn't?"

"I heard a woman who would love nothing more than to find out she had a grandchild so she isn't totally alone in this world at an age when life will only be taking bit by bit everything she has left. That's what I heard."

Adam's voice was so soft Myron almost couldn't hear him. "Yeah, and what happens if all we find out is that we aren't related? That it's just a stupid coincidence Joe and I look alike?"

"There is that," Myron acknowledged.

*****

The next morning, Myron announced he was going to get the hampers from the back so he could soak the laundry needing to be sanitized while he was doing the cleaning.

Adam gave him a hard look as he disappeared out the door. This was Myron's way of forcing him to get the hampers out of the front hall. The guy might look and act mild, but Adam occasionally caught a glimpse of something very tough in Myron's core.

In the front hall, Adam pulled the hampers out. He glanced toward Mary's door. It was open. He realized he badly wanted to see the photo of the dead man with his face again.

He eased down the hallway to peer in. Although he was careful to stand back from the open door, Mary spotted him instantly from where she was seated in a slipper chair.

"Please come in," she said as she closed the book she had been reading. The large cross on the front identified it as her Bible. She set it aside. As if drawn by a magnet, Adam advanced until he could view the picture up close.

Mary watched him without speaking.

"What was he like?" Adam asked suddenly.

"Joe was a charming, funny, loving drifter."

Adam looked at Mary, surprised.

"My Joe loved new things, experiences, people; then he would suddenly get bored and move on to the next thing that caught his eye. He spent all his thirty-four years treating life like an enormous buffet—sampling everything but committing to nothing."

"How did he die?"

"Fell asleep at the wheel and plowed into a concrete retainer wall. The impact crushed his chest."

"Did he know his dad?"

The unexpected question startled Mary. "Of course he did. Joe was seventeen when Chris—his father and my husband—died. Chris was at the courthouse when he had a heart attack. They told us he was dead before he hit the floor."

"Courthouse?"

"He was a lawyer."

Adam nodded.

"What about your dad?"

His jaw muscle bunched. "I better be getting back to work," he said by way of answer.

Mary nodded. "Of course."

Chapter 15

T he three teens hadn't made it to the stairs leading to their rooms in Pittison House when Jarett called to them from the door of the office.

"There's another letter to the editor in the newspaper concerning the care center," he said waving the paper.

All three veered immediately toward him. He handed the paper to Myron.

Myron sat down in the easy chair while Adam and Soosie leaned over his shoulders.

After last week's letter to the editor, it appears Soda Springs Care Center was able to complete the painting of the building through the efforts of three young people under what may be a violation of the child labor laws since they still looked to be in their teens.

Regardless, the grave concern is what is being allowed to occur inside the center.

Recently, it was observed one of the residents is morbidly obese. She is allowed to sit on the front porch alone without anyone present to prevent her from wandering off. It is obvious by her girth she is being allowed to eat herself into a state where her heart will give out from straining against such fat. It makes one wonder what kind of junk these people are being forced to consume daily.

It was also observed another of the residents is permitted to smoke on the front porch, again jeopardizing his health and the health of those who find it necessary to walk in the vicinity of his polluting second-hand smoke.

This writer has also noted several residents who are allowed to leave the premises and wander through the community without a caregiver being present to ensure their safety and the safety of the community. So the question is, Soda Springs, how much longer is this community going to allow the mistreatment and maltreatment occurring at the care center before taking action to protect the vulnerable persons who have too long been trapped in this untenable situation? Adah Skelton.

Myron lowered the paper, and the three teens exchanged looks of disbelief.

"So?" Jarett asked.

"What a total crock," Adam said.

"Complete bullshit," Soosie added.

Myron just shook his head as he folded the paper and handed it back to Jarett.

"Okay," Jarett said, "but I want you three to know if this continues to escalate, we're going to pull you out. I appreciate that Mrs. Fuentes is willing to work with us, but not if it means any of you end up being damaged in any way. Now, go change. Dinner will be happening soon."

*****

"Is that woman whacked or what?" Adam asked when he returned from changing his clothes.

Myron was carefully tucking in his polo shirt and fastening his pants. "She's mean and creepy. Remember when I said she started stalking the family? Well, she was really stalking the little kids in the family. She was showing up at the grade school trying to get them to talk about what went on at their homes.

"The one thing all of us Tatums are trained to do from the time we're in diapers is to tell our folks about anyone who is asking questions about the family because kids can't always spot undercover cops or snitches, so of course the kids went home and let their folks know some old lady was getting in their faces about the family. Because she made sure not to identify herself, it took a while before the family was able to figure out who was behind the interrogations Eventually, one of the kids spotted her sitting in the window at the Cottage Café having dinner and pointed her out."

"So what'd the family do?"

"They just took turns tailing her everywhere she went. She parked, a Tatum parked. She got out, a Tatum got out and watched her."

"Bet she was torqued big time."

"She was howling for police protection within three days."

"Did she get it?"

"Nah. Chief Braden talked to Uncle Ralph and some of the kids. He apparently told her he appreciated her efforts to clean up Soda Springs, but she was crossing the line by talking to the kids without a parent or guardian. If she continued, he might have to charge her. Of course, then she changed her focus to trying to get the chief fired."

"What is it, payback every time someone tells her she is out of line?"

"Pretty much, from everything I've heard."

Chapter 16

David was on the front porch with a cup of coffee in one hand and a cigar in the other, basking in the morning sun, when the kids arrived at the center.

"Could you smell my smoke when you got off the bus?" he asked.

All three shook their heads.

"Damn, gonna have to get me a bigger stogie if I'm gonna to kill the population of Soda Springs with secondhand smoke," he said. "You saw yesterday's letter to the editor?"

They all nodded.

"Just shows you how stone-cold mean Adah is, talking about Bert like she did. Adah knows what happened; the newspaper was all over it." He drew on his cigar again before going on. "Believe me, if Bert had her druthers, she would have retired from the library rather than having a blood vessel rupture in her brain leaving her with the cognitive function of a small child. The only thing she has to make her happy is food. And if she dies of obesity, well, damn, she'll die happy." He flicked the ashes from his cigar over the railing. "You are pretty pathetic when the only thing you can find to do is screw with the lives of a bunch of short-timers who are only waiting to age out of this life. She probably spends her spare time strangling small animals." He waved the kids inside.

Olivia was just parking Bert at the dining room table when the kids clocked in. Bert smiled happily at them like they were the best thing she had seen in her life.

Olivia followed them down the hall. "Just want you kids to know I'm madder than a mule with a mouth full of bumblebees, so if'n I get a bit short, it isn't at you. It's cuz this place is being haunted by the old witch out there. She's just upsetting everyone when they should be enjoying whatever days the Good Lord is planning on providing them."

"What's the worst that can happen?" Soosie asked.

"Why, we could get closed down, sugar, if Adah can convince the state there really are bad things happening here and she sure seems bent on it."

"What would happen to everybody who lives here?"

"They'd be sent to live at different places, and it would be just like breaking up a family. Oh, they fuss and squabble like any family, but they also depend on each other, look out for each other. They think of this place as their home—their last home. Take them out of here and stick them in a new place with new people, new routines, new staff—it'd likely be the end of most of them real quick." Shaking her head, Olivia took off down the hall.

Of the three young faces scattering to gather laundry hampers, Adam's was the most troubled. Somewhere in the last few days, he had discovered a miniscule bit of hope. Hope for what he hadn't figured out, but it was connected to the man in the picture and by extension this place, which housed the woman to whom the picture belonged.

*****

Myron was damp-mopping the main room when Emily and Mary returned from their morning walk.

The two women were a study in contrasts. Although both were tall, Emily would have been described as rangy, while Mary would have been considered willowy. Emily was dressed in her usual outfit of jeans, faded tee-shirt, and Birkenstocks. Mary wore trim navy-blue slacks and a striped top. Her feet were neatly shod in canvas slip-ons. When she spotted Myron, Emily strode in his direction while Mary followed in her wake.

"Em, please. This may not be appropriate," Mary said.

Emily just ignored her as she positioned herself in front of Myron and held out her hand. "Hi, I'm Emily. And you're Myron, right?"

He nodded as he shook her hand.

"You're familiar with the small mystery we have in which your coworker is the spitting image of Mary's son?"

Myron nodded a bit more warily.

"Do you know anything about his father? Have you seen a picture? Heard him talk about his father?"

"No, ma'am."

She studied him. "You know, I spent over forty years teaching in the sea of hormones that passes for the college freshman year. You develop a sixth sense about truth-telling when you have heard probably a million excuses about everything from missing assignments to absences, so I know you are telling the truth, but you're not telling all of it."

"It's not mine to tell," he answered simply.

*****

"Mary watched you the whole time we ate lunch even though you had your back to her," Soosie commented to Adam as the they headed back to the laundry room with Myron.

Adam shrugged and then something snicked through the fog he had been carrying since Saturday. "No," Adam said. "She was watching Joe, not me."

The little bit of something that had welled up collapsed. He was just the animated picture of a dead man. Nothing had really changed; he himself still didn't matter. He began pulling wet sheets out of the washer and loading them into the dryer.

*****

Climbing on the bus at the end of the work day, the threesome didn't pay attention to the blue Altima pulling out and following the bus as it made its way across town. When they disembarked at the bus stop, the car's driver held up her cell phone, looking at the pictures she had taken on Saturday and compared them to the three walking down the street. She edged her car along while following them. When they turned into the walk leading to the Pittison House, she snapped pictures until they disappeared through the door.

Chapter 17

Jarett was waiting when the three teens walked into Pittison House at the end of the day. "Soosie, I need to talk to you for minute," he said. She answered by crossing her arms over her chest and hunching her shoulders defensively as she followed him to the office.

Adam and Myron looked at each other as the office door closed and then headed upstairs. They had just reached the door of their room when they heard Soosie's voice start shrieking, "No! No! No!" and the door to the office slam open.

Myron was already leaping down the stairs with Adam following. There was a blur of pink as Soosie raced by, flung open the front door, and disappeared down the steps.

Myron was poised to go after her when Adam grabbed his arm. "What are you doing?" he asked.

Myron looked at Jarett. "Don't let her do anything stupid," was all Jarett said.

Myron shook out of Adam's grasp and bounded out the door. Stopping at the sidewalk, he looked both ways before spotting Soosie's pink scrubs. He took after her, his long legs rapidly closing the distance between them. When he was close enough, he called her name.

She glanced back and then cut across the street onto the gravel road leading to a small park tucked down the side of a hill. She stopped so abruptly Myron almost ran her over.

Catching his breath, he watched the rise and fall of Soosie's shoulders until they begin to slow as her breathing normalized. Suddenly she swung around, her hand raised. Myron caught her wrist, and when she swung with her other hand, he caught it as well. She struggled against him as he held her; his grip was too strong to break.

Keeping his firm hold, he pushed her until the back of her knees met with the edge of a bench, and she sat down abruptly. When he felt the fight in her collapsing, he released her hands. Tears began to stream down her face.

He squatted in front of her, watching.

Like a small child frustrated to find herself crying, she shoved the heels of her hands into her eyes and rubbed. "Sammy's gone. She signed off on him, and now he's gone forever. I'll never see him again."

Myron pulled out a paper towel he had stuffed in his pocket at work and pushed it into her hand. She wiped her eyes, then fidgeted with it. She raised her eyes to the sky and gulped in air.

"Who's Sammy?" Myron asked softly.

"My nephew," she said as the tears threatened to start again. Suddenly she gave a short, harsh laugh. "*My* nephew, who is some relation to you."

Myron looked startled, then a flash of comprehension crossed his face.

Words began to tumble out of Soosie. "Everything went to hell after my dad had his accident. My mom was so stressed the doctor prescribed her pills to help her cope, which was kinda funny since my dad was a pharmacist and always talking about people getting addicted to meds. Well, Mom did—and in a big way. They didn't just help her cope; they were a way of her checking out entirely, which was perfect for Stevie to fly completely out of control. My sister always liked the bad boys, so when Mom was zonked out, Stevie went hunting for the baddest she could find."

"A Tatum."

"Yeah, a Tatum. Tyler Tatum to be exact."

Myron looked down and nodded.

"I guess it doesn't take much to figure out they were screwing around while doing drugs, alcohol, whatever and whenever. Just about the time Dad died, she announced she was pregnant. Naturally, Tyler pulled a Houdini and vanished."

Myron shook his head. No Tatum ever left a baby behind. It was one of those rules his family lived by. If you didn't do your duty as the father, then your child might grow up to be law-abiding, and that would not be good for maintaining the family image. "No. Tyler didn't intentionally abandon his baby."

"Oh, yeah? Funny how nobody has seen him since the big announcement."

"It's because he hasn't been around. He was at some party in Salem when a guy manhandled the girl he was with. Tyler ended up stabbing him. He's been in jail for two years." Another Tatum rule: If you're dumb enough to get caught, don't call for bail.

"You mean he's in jail for protecting my sister?"

"I guess. You'll have to ask her about it."

Soosie shook her head. "She's in jail too. I put her there."

Myron looked at her surprised. "You put your sister in jail?"

"Kinda. See, when Sammy was born, his head and brain hadn't formed properly. He has microcephaly, probably due to the drugs and booze she was doing. He's the sweetest baby, but obviously he has developmental issues. I came home one day and caught her beating Sammy with an effin' broom handle!" Her face reflected the white-hot fury that had surged through her. "I wanted nothing more than to kill her. Neighbors reported the fight to the police. I went to juvie for beating up on her, while she went to jail for child abuse. The state took Sammy. Now, because of some plea deal, she signed off on him so he can be adopted." She sounded bereft.

"I'm sorry. Losing someone you love is one of the shittiest things that can happen to anyone." A silent agony passed over Myron's face.

The snark edged back into Soosie's voice. "Oh, yeah? What would you know about it?"

He stood up and stared into the space over her head. "A lot," he whispered. He turned and walked away from her.

Soosie sat for a long time, her thoughts piling up like the clouds beginning to build along the western horizon. And like the clouds, her thoughts jumbled and collided against each other, producing nothing but a downpour of frustration, anger, and sadness. Her plan for getting out of the system and reclaiming Sammy was blown, and her heart was broken.

Eventually the warm spring air chilled as the clouds pushed across the Coast Range into the valley. Soosie rubbed her arms. There was nothing she could do except head back to the Pitt.

Jarett had apparently been listening for the front door's bell, monitoring the comings and goings of the residents, because he stepped out of the office as soon as she entered.

"Glad you're back," he said and then looked over her shoulder. "Where's Myron?"

She shrugged. "Don't know."

"Didn't he catch up with you?"

"Yeah, but then he took off," she answered, her tone indicating she could care less about Myron.

"Your dinner's in the fridge." The slight chilliness in Jarett's voice let her know he was guessing she was probably responsible for Myron's absence.

Heading upstairs to change, she saw Adam standing in the doorway to his and Myron's room, watching her. He abruptly turned into it and closed the door.

As she climbed the second staircase leading to the floor with her room, a whiff of concern flitted through her. Once she closed the door to her room, she told herself Myron was a big boy, and he could take care of himself, and if he couldn't, well, he still wasn't her problem. But a trace of uneasiness remained.

When she finally made it back down to the kitchen, she found two plates in the refrigerator—one with her name and one with Myron's. She didn't bother to nuke her food, just ate it cold off the plate while leaning against the counter. When she had finished, she rinsed her plate and added it to the load in the dishwasher. Rain began to tap against the windows. She had not heard the front door chime.

She went to her room and picked up *Stranger in a Strange Land*, but her thoughts kept straying. The small tear-streaked face of her nephew with his little hands reaching for her as the paramedics carried him out kept arising unbidden in her brain. She had promised him she would come for him. She would bring him home and keep him safe. Except now, she could never keep her promise. He had been swallowed by the system and lost to her forever. The longer she let those thoughts careen around in her head, the more on edge she became.

Finally, she crept out of her room and down the stairs before sitting down where she could see the second floor landing. She really didn't care if Myron made it back or not, but waiting and watching would provide a distraction even the book could not give her at this moment.

The clock was nearing seven p.m. when Myron came through the door. Soosie saw Jarett stride out of the office. She was too far away to hear clearly what was being said; however, Jarett looked pissed when he confronted the soaked teenager.

★ ★ ★ ★ ★

"Where the hell have you been? Soosie got back hours ago."

"I went to the cemetery," Myron said.

"The cemetery's way out of town. How'd you get there?"

"Walked, sir."

"Geez, man, what's at the cemetery?"

Myron's reply was barely audible. "My sister."

Jarett opened his mouth and then closed it. "Go get a hot shower and get yourself dried off. Dinner's in the refrig." He turned away and then turned back. "Next time you want to go, tell us first and we'll drive you, got it?"

Myron ducked his head.

At the top of the stairs, Adam waited with a pile of Myron's clothes in his hands. "You are so not going to drip all over my bed," he said. "I'll heat up your dinner."

"So where did you really go, man?" Adam asked when they were safely behind their closed door.

"I went to the cemetery, just like I said," Myron answered, omitting mention of the other stop he had made on his way there.

"Why?"

"I haven't been there since I got put here, and I wanted to see Lucy."

"Who's Lucy?"

"She was my little sister. The fiercest, most stubborn, independent little sister in the history of the world," he said. He touched a small half-moon-shaped scar close to his right eye. "She clocked me with one of my own trucks for making her get out of my stuff." He smiled at the memory. "But then she stopped being constant trouble. They found leukemia when she was four."

He closed his eyes. "The only way Mom could cope was by drinking. The last time, Mom had a bottle hidden in her bag. She kept going off to the restroom. As she got drunker and drunker, she got louder and louder. Finally the nurses told Dad he had to get her out of there."

He opened his eyes and looked at Adam. "Have you ever been to Doernbecher Children's Hospital?"

Adam shook his head.

"Well, it's a monster of a place. You have to take elevators, cross through OHSU, and go forever to reach the kids' cancer ward, plus we'd ended up parking a long ways away. Mom didn't wanna leave, so she fought Dad. He finally half-carried, half-dragged her out while I stayed with Lucy. When they were gone, I climbed up in her bed and held her. It was such a scary place, and she was so little." His voice was thick with remembrance. "She died before Dad got back."

"How old were you?"

"Ten."

Chapter 18

The next morning, Soosie waited until Myron left the laundry room with his cleaning caddy. As soon as she thought he was out of earshot, she asked Adam where Myron had gone when he had left her. The faint disdain in her voice provoked Adam to answer with an almost physical bluntness.

"The cemetery to see his sister."

"Sister?" Her voice wavered with surprise.

"His five-year-old sister who died of leukemia in his arms when he was ten years old and alone with her. So, yeah, you're not the only one with a lock on loss and grief."

Adam could tell he had finally knocked her off-center. He grabbed his caddy and walked out the door with a sense of providing a little vindication for Myron.

At lunch, Soosie was the last to set her tray at the table. The two males ate just the way they did at the Pitt, with their heads down and no eye contact. Reaching for her glass of ice tea, she suddenly noticed Myron's hands. They were big hands with long, slender fingers. The kind of hands artists had. The kind of hands her father had. The connection jolted her. She felt Myron's hands on her wrists again. They were strong, too strong for her to wrest out of, but he hadn't hurt her either. Indeed, there had been gentleness in his grip.

She hastily set down her drink and grabbed her fork. Her mind was going places she didn't like. Before it could travel too far along an unwanted path, Emily's voice caught her attention; it caught all their attention. The three teens listened closely as they ate.

"David, you have been in Soda Springs since God was a boy, so what is the deal with Adah Skelton? I mean, why does she have this raging need to destroy things she really doesn't know jack shit about and aren't about her anyway?"

David wiped his mouth. "Because she was raised with a sense of entitlement approximately the size of Mount Hood, and if anyone crosses her, she brings out the chainsaws and flamethrowers to remind them they are dealing with someone who can't be touched because of their importance."

"Elucidate."

"When her father bought the newspaper back in the late fifties, he assumed ownership gave him carte blanche to run everyone else's life in Soda Springs. He wielded printer's ink like a truncheon on the innocent and guilty alike. He played this game where he would print a damaging story, then when challenged, he would print a tiny little retraction buried somewhere in the back of the paper. A lot of fine people were hurt, some irreparably, because of his poison.

"During the time they owned the paper, Adah's mom thought she was some kind of high society and always dressed to the nines. She muscled her way onto every committee and woman's group in town by subtly threatening them with 'exposure' if they didn't include her and, of course, immediately elect her to the top position. She liked to brag that she set the tone for all of Soda Springs society, as if Soda Springs even had a society that didn't basically revolve around bull semen and field crops exclusively.

"Adah was well-schooled in her family's Machiavellian ways as Aldus and Doris's spoiled-brat daughter. The elder Skeltons may be gone, but Adah has made it her life mission to carry on their fine tradition of spreading destruction far and wide, especially for those she has decided have slighted her in some way."

"Just how far do you think she is going to go in trying to shut us down?" Emily asked.

David shook his head. "What happened here cost her the last link she had with the newspaper, the last link with anyone remembering who she had been. I wouldn't put it past her to burn this place down with all of us in it if she can't convince the state to shut down the center."

"So pretty much, we're gonna get screwed one way or another," Paul said as he hitched up the strap on his pink sundress.

"Are we going to get to choose where we go, or will the state make the decision if they close this place down?" Mary asked.

"I suspect we're going to get placed based on what we can afford to pay, so our choices are going to be limited to whatever almshouses have room," David answered.

Clarence began to make his nonsensical sounds and frantically wave his arm around. Steve abruptly got up, balancing himself on his crutches. "Anyone know where Olivia or Lidiya are? Clarence needs his afternoon siesta."

Myron stood and deposited his tray on the trolley. "I can take Clarence back," he said.

He positioned himself behind Clarence's chair and pushed, guiding it away from the table and towards the hall. Soosie watched the muscles in his broad shoulders flex with the effort of maneuvering the large chair and its occupant. Adam blocked her view when he deposited his tray on the trolley.

Adam glanced at Mary's face as he passed the large table. She looked stricken. Adam remembered seeing the same look on his own face reflected in wet windows as he made his way to the laundromat the night he was ejected.

*****

Steve swung along behind Myron and Clarence. "If you can get the chair positioned, I'll find somebody to help get him into bed."

"I helped my mom into bed all the time, sir," Myron said, "and she's bigger than Clarence. I think I can manage."

"Your mom disabled?" Steve asked.

"Alcoholic."

Steve nodded. "Same thing."

Myron positioned the chair and pushed it upright. Using his foot to brace Clarence's slippered feet, he reached under the skeletal man's arms and interlaced his fingers against the man's protruding backbone. In one smooth motion, Myron lifted the man, pivoted, and sat him on the bed.

Steve put a crutch tip against the seat of the chair and shoved to move it out of Myron's way.

Slipping his arms under Clarence's legs and behind him, Myron lifted and settled the man on his bed. Steve balanced himself as he pulled up the blankets before sitting down next to Clarence.

Clarence once again began to make sounds as he waved his one partially mobile arm around. Steve patted his chest. "Whoa, whoa, man," he said. "Nobody's gonna separate us, okay? We go as a unit, just like we did before. And this time we stay as a unit. Got it? I'm always gonna be here for you. I'm not leaving you behind for the enemy."

Clarence answered with a little whimper.

Steve looked at Myron. "If it isn't too much trouble, could you get me a cup of coffee?" He grinned behind his beard. "I make a terrible mess when I carry it myself, and Elena has threatened me with KP duty if I don't cut it out."

"Do you take anything in it?"

"Just black." He looked back at Clarence. The man's eyes watched him anxiously. "Give me a couple minutes, and then meet me at the dining room table."

Myron had just placed the coffee on the now-emptied table when he heard Steve's crutches in the hall. Myron waited until he swung into the dining room.

Steve dropped into a chair and pulled a nearby chair close to rest his stump on.

"All this talk of this place being shut down is worrying Clarence to death, and death is exactly the route he'll take if he thinks he's going be hauled out of here without me. He blew it the first time. He won't screw it up a second time."

"Pardon, sir?"

"Have you noticed the side of his head?"

Myron nodded.

"Shot himself a few years back. Bullet took most everything but his memories and his life. Ironic, huh, because those were the two things he was trying to escape." Steve took a sip of coffee. "Vietnam War mean anything to you?"

Myron nodded. "Yes, sir. A great-uncle of mine was there. He didn't come home."

"A lot of men and women didn't come home. And a lot of the rest who did wished later they had died in one of those godforsaken muddy paddies, because what waited back here was just about as bad.

"Clarence and I met in Vietnam, 1964. We were young, invincible, and gung-ho. Nine months later we were none of those things. Like everyone else, we were doing everything we could to stay alive and get home. It was the thought driving us every day and night. We were just weeks away when I stepped on a punji stick. Know what that is?"

Myron shook his head.

"A devil's tool used by the Viet Cong. It was bamboo stakes covered with toxic material, like venom or feces, hidden in the vegetation. They could pierce boots. It went right through the canvas on my boot and into my ankle. The wound itself wasn't too bad until infection set in.

"Four days later, I'm out of my head with fever, and Clarence had to cut me out of my boot. He got me medevacked out. I ended up at Letterman Army Hospital. Tony Bennett might have left his heart in San Francisco, but I left my leg.

"I didn't see Clarence again for forty-eight years. Tried looking for him a few times, but it didn't amount to much. Always liked to imagine he made it home, found a pretty little chick to marry, and was living the dream.

"Then one day, I get a call from the veteran's hospital in Portland. They had found an old Polaroid photo somebody took when we first arrived in 'Nam among Clarence's stuff when he was brought in. It had my name and serial number on it. They tracked me down through my own VA medical records. They were trying to find information about his family after he shot himself. What was in the old records led to dead-ends, literally.

"I did some checking through some of the Vietnam veterans' associations and stuff. Best we could figure out was Clarence had been one of those veterans who could never mesh back into society. Drifted around all those years in a fog of drugs and alcohol. Don't establish too many permanent connections living like that. So there wasn't anyone. Just me.

"Truth is, I didn't have anyone either. Couple of divorces, no kids. My folks gone. When he regained consciousness, I told Clarence we'd move in together somewhere. I'd take care of him. Between his condition and our incomes, Elena was the only one who threw the door open to us."

"He doesn't have access to a gun again, does he?"

Steve's face was somber. "All he would have to do is quit eating, son. You just picked him up, so you know there's not much left of him. It wouldn't take too many days before he would be able to finish the job he attempted four years ago."

Steve drifted off into his own thoughts, and Myron slipped away to the laundry room.

Chapter 19

That night Myron and Adam carried armloads of their own clothes to the basement. Dropping them on the floor in front of the washer and dryer, they sorted them into piles. Myron tossed their underwear and scrubs in the washer. When the machine began filling, he pulled an old, discolored plastic chair out of the debris stacked along the wall and placed it next to the one Adam was occupying.

"Think it's safe?" he asked as he wobbled the chair around.

"If your ass hits the floor, it's not," Adam replied.

They sat quietly listening to the water filling the machine. When it clicked over to the agitation cycle, Myron asked. "So what happens after you're out of here?"

Adam shrugged. "No clue, man. Hell, I don't even know where I'm going to live come September."

"Is that when you age out?"

Adam nodded.

"Don't suppose you can go back to your family."

Adam threw a disbelieving look Myron's way. "They tossed me at fifteen, so it's a pretty sure bet they would not open the door when I'm eighteen." He looked at the floor. "I doubt they even remember I exist."

The washing machine sloshed for a few moments. "When do you exit?" Adam finally asked.

"July."

"You gonna go home then?"

Myron looked troubled. "I could. I just don't know if I should. There'll be a lot of pressure to become a full-on participant in the family. I so do not want to do that. I don't want to spend the rest of my life looking over my shoulder to see if that is the day I go down. I don't want any kids I might have to spend their lives dodging and ducking blowback from stuff that happens but they had no control over it. I don't want to be ashamed to say my name. I don't want people to assume I am automatically a bad guy because much of my family is."

Myron got up to shift the wash into the dryer and push the next load in. When he came back to sit beside Adam, he put his elbow on his knee and rested his chin in his hand. "Funny, the care center is the only place I have ever been in this town where people didn't freak out about my family."

Adam nodded. "I kinda got the feeling today from what was said at lunch you Tatums may not be as scary as you think, especially compared to this Adah Skelton. She's got them spooked bad."

"What's got them spooked is they have no idea what will happen to them if the state comes in and yanks their home out from under them."

The knuckles on Adam's interlaced fingers went white. "Yeah, it's kinda tough when the future is just a big dark hole."

* * * * *

In the night, the dream returned to Adam. Once again the darkness stretched beyond the last bit of light. It felt huge, a giant, black empty space filled with teeth waiting to devour him. It brought him upright with a sharp cry.

Myron's sleepy voice came out of the dark. "Adam? You okay?"

"Yeah, man. Just a stupid dream that shows up once in a while. Sorry to wake you."

There was just enough light in the room for Myron to catch the outline of Adam dropping back on his bed and rolling over on his side. He listened for Adam's breathing. It did not settle back into sleep.

Myron wondered what kind of dream it was. The sound Adam had made when he sat up was like a terrified child.

Flipping onto his back, Myron stared in the darkness. He thought about what it would be like to never have had a birthday, a Christmas, even enough food at times. He might be a member of the town's most notorious family, but they were a family in the deepest sense of the word. He had never done without and never would as long as any of them were still kicking. That, too, was part of their family code.

He turned his head to look over at Adam's bed. The Pitt was all Adam had left, and by September, he wouldn't even have that. Myron couldn't even imagine how scared he must feel.

Chapter 20

Despite the clear, bright light streaming through the windows into the care center, the air felt heavier and darker than usual. It wasn't the somber quiet that had awaited them the morning Meryl died. This carried a subtle dusting of tension and fear.

Olivia came out of Bert's room with an armload of bedding she dumped in the hall hamper. Spotting the trio at the time clock, she waved for them to hold up for her.

"Just want to let you know we're gonna to be needing y'all to help out today. I guess you noticed Elena wasn't here yesterday. Arturo's back got really bad, and she had to take him to the emergency room. They're sending him for an MRI and some other tests today, but it is looking like he's going to need surgery about as fast as they can get him scheduled."

"Of course."

"Sure."

"Just let us know."

"You're right good people." Olivia smiled as she turned back down the hall.

Soosie followed her. She had finished two of the books she'd borrowed and was going to slip them onto Emily's desk before starting the work day.

She was surprised when she peeked in the room to see both Emily and Mary sitting and sipping coffee.

"I'm sorry," she said. "I thought you would be on your walk. I just wanted to return a couple of the books."

"This time of year, we usually walk quite early when the air is still cool. Come in, dear," Emily said.

Soosie stepped in to set the books on the corner of Emily's desk.

"Are you ready for more?"

Soosie shook her head. "I still have the LeGuin books. Thank you, though."

Mary tilted her head. "How long are you required to live at the Pittison?" she asked.

Soosie shrugged. "It's different for each kid. Some are only there for a few days. Others are there until they turn eighteen and age out."

"Will you be going home soon?"

She shook her head. "No. I'm one of the ones that will age out, along with Adam and Myron."

"How long have you three lived there?" Emily asked.

"I came in January. I think Myron was there a couple of months before me, and Adam has been there a few years."

Startled, Mary asked, "Why so long?"

"Guess he didn't have any other options. He told David on our first day here he didn't know who his father was. I don't know about his mom. Other than Myron, he doesn't deal much with anyone."

"What happens to you when you 'age out' of the Pittison?" Emily asked.

"The Pitt closes our files, and we're on our own."

"But where do you go to live? How do feed yourselves? Get what you need?" Mary inquired.

"Not sure." Although her shrug was casual, Soosie's eyes were troubled as she slipped out of the room.

Walking back to the laundry room, she realized she had never even wondered why Adam had been stuck in the Pitt for so long.

Adam was unloading towels from the washer into the dryer when Soosie entered the laundry room. Her glance skimmed over him as it usually did, but she stopped when she realized, although she saw him every day, she had always avoided actually looking at him.

Pulling her cleaning caddy out of the cupboard, she set it on the other side of the table and pretended to check the contents. She surreptitiously studied Adam as he punched the power button on the dryer. Adam was actually good looking: tall with gray-blue eyes, thick blonde hair, and broad shoulders. If they were all still in high school instead of the laundry room in a care center, he would have been one of the guys the girls would definitely have the hots for.

It also suddenly occurred to her she had never actually seen him smile or laugh. It was like he was always hunkered down behind this really thick wall.

She looked down when he came around to grab his cleaning caddy and head out the door. She picked up hers and followed thoughtfully.

*****

Adam helped load the food trays on the trolley and return it to the kitchen. He had begun wiping down the tables and chairs in the dining room when Mary walked up. She stood for a minute watching him work. He didn't look at her or acknowledge her presence until she pulled a chair out at the table he was cleaning and sat down. It startled him enough he actually looked at her.

"Good morning, Adam," she smiled. She gestured to the chair opposite her. "Do you mind sitting a minute?"

He looked at the cloth in his hand, avoiding her eyes.

"Trust me, Elena won't mind if I take a few minutes of your time." She gestured to the chair opposite her again. "Please."

Adam pulled it out and sat down.

"I understand you have lived at the Pittison House for several years."

Adam flicked her a glance and nodded.

"Do you know any of the history behind Pittison House?"

He gave a slight head shake.

"When Oscar Pittison was fourteen years old, he was put in the streets by his family."

Adam looked up at her in surprise.

"It wasn't uncommon back in those days. Families were usually quite large and money quite short. Older children were sent out to start making their way so there would be enough for the younger ones.

"Usually, these young men would ask around until they found a place they could apprentice. There they would learn the skills they needed to move up in the world. That was what Mr. Pittison did, except no one would take him on. He had a speech impediment people equated with being mentally slow.

"Finally, a man named Abe Warbels found him asleep in a sawdust pile behind his lumber yard. Abe took him in, fed him, and gave him a place to sleep and a job. Mr. Pittison learned the business thoroughly. He took over running the lumberyard and eventually bought the business from Warbels.

"Far from being slow, Mr. Pittison was a very shrewd businessman who amassed a great deal of money. It was then he built his mansion, Pittison House.

"Even with all his money, he never forgot what it was like to be cold and hungry, and have nobody care. Mr. Pittison and his wife didn't have any children of their own, but they opened their door to any young person in need. Kids of all ages were housed, fed, clothed, and given an opportunity to learn a trade or advance their education.

"Mr. Pittison had this philosophy. He said every kid is like a plant. In addition to the rain, they need some sunshine to blossom. He made it his life's mission to be the sunshine."

She paused as David rolled into the room. He looked them over. "Everything okay?" he asked.

"It will be as soon as you bug out," Mary replied evenly.

David nodded, stuck his unlit cigar in his mouth, and said, "Gone." He rolled to the door and pushed the button to open it.

As soon as David was out the door, Mary looked back at Adam. "I always thought that was a cool idea. Something tells me you have probably had more than your fair share of rain. I would very much like to be able to offer some sunshine, if you will let me."

She let the thought settle for a moment.

"And, Adam, it isn't because you look like Joe." She paused. "Okay, maybe it is a little. I suppose the resemblance makes me think I know you on some level. However, please understand, I am not trying to use you to bring Joe back. You two are as different as chalk and cheese. He was an explosion of confetti everywhere he went. You are like a ghost in the room."

Adam sat stone still, shoulders hunched, looking down at the cloth in his hands.

"I just find something compelling in the fact that a young man begins working at Soda Springs Care Center, my home, who bears an uncanny resemblance to my deceased son. Perhaps life has maneuvered us to this moment because we have the means to help each other be…less alone.

"But regardless, the call is yours. We can try to get to know each other and see where it goes, or we can leave everything as it is."

Adam looked at her, unaware she saw his tremendous longing to connect behind roiling clouds of distrust, nor, that at that moment, he supplanted the dead in her heart.

Mary smiled at him as she got up. "I'll let you get back to your work."

Chapter 21

The day proceeded in a blur as all three teens worked hard to get their jobs done while being constantly called on to provide assistance to Olivia and Lidiya. But Mary's words circled Adam's thoughts continuously.

On the bus ride home, he stared out the window. Myron glanced at him now and again, but remained silent. Whatever struggle was going on in his roommate was almost palpable.

As soon as the three teens walked through the front door, they could smell pizza cooking. They passed Jarett, who was coming out of the room set aside for common activities.

"Movie tonight," he said.

After dinner, the young people gathered in the common room. Although there had been seven residents in the morning, two of the kids had been moved out during the day. That left the three older teens and the two younger girls who shared the third floor with Soosie.

Myron and Adam sat on the long couch. They were joined by the two younger teen girls. Soosie flung herself in the dilapidated recliner.

"I just love this movie," Alesha said. "I saw it when it first came out."

"Is this the one about the two kids who have cancer and one of them dies at the end?" Chelsea asked.

"Yeah. It is so good."

Myron abruptly got up from the couch and left the room.

Jarett, who was just positioning the DVD in the player, looked at Adam. "Bad choice?" he asked.

"For some."

Alesha immediately began to protest. "No. It is awesome."

"Maybe it's not awesome when you actually watch someone you love die from cancer," Soosie said sharply.

Both younger girls turned to look at Soosie, their faces duplicate blanks.

"It doesn't sound like my kind of movie," Adam said. He got up to follow Myron back to their room.

Soosie stayed put. The movie was depressing, shmoopy, and illuminating.

* * * * *

Whatever was weighing on Adam's mind didn't diminish over the rest of the weekend. By late Sunday afternoon, he was edgy and restless, moving around their small room and then leaving to cruise the rest of the house, and then coming back to the bedroom.

Finally, Myron blocked his umpteenth trip out the door. "You are giving me anxiety with all this perpetual motion. Maybe you could try something else, like talk about it?"

Adam flopped back onto his bed. "It's Mary." Just saying her name opened a spillway of words and emotions as he poured out Friday's conversation.

"So Mary is interested in, maybe, trying to establish a relationship with you? Am I right?" Myron asked.

Adam nodded. "Pretty much."

"And the problem is you don't want to?"

"No, I do. At least I think I do…but maybe I don't. I don't know."

"You're scared."

Adam reared up, opening his mouth to protest, then stopped. Instead, he nodded. "Scared shitless. I've never had anyone even pretend to care whether I lived or died."

"I care," Myron protested. "I don't need a dead roommate stinking up the room."

"Very funny."

"Actually, I do get it. In school I would make a friend. It would last until somebody figured out who my family was, and then I was drop-kicked pretty fast. It's a little strange since we've only been roommates for three weeks, but you're like the longest friend I've ever had who I wasn't related to. And yes, I do care."

"Well, you're pretty much it."

"No, I'm not. From what you've said, Mr. Orenco cared about you. Chief Braden cared enough to make sure you were at least physically safe all those years. And Soosie…"

Adam cast a disbelieving look at Myron.

"Okay, not Soosie. But I think Mary does care, or at least wants to care, if you let her. But, dude, you have a wall high enough to keep out a whole battalion of orcs. You're gonna need to trust enough to make at least a little opening in it."

"And if it doesn't work out?"

"It definitely won't work out if you don't give it a chance."

Chapter 22

The trio was lined up Monday morning and running their name badges through the time clock when Emily and Mary came through the front door.

Although Emily turned toward the hall, Mary stopped with her eyes on Adam.

There was an awkward split second before Emily smoothly said, "I'll get our coffee." She gestured to Soosie. "Since we're heading in the same direction, maybe you can let me know how you like the books so far."

Myron followed Soosie and Emily down the hall. In a heartbeat, only Mary and Adam stood in the entry area.

Adam was rigid with tension, his eyes fixed on the floor. Mary waited silently. Finally, Adam drew a shaky breath and looked at her. "I'm in," he said.

Mary's smile was like sunshine. "Thank you," she said softly.

He squirmed, rubbing his hands on his scrub pants and keeping his eyes cast down. Finally he made a helpless gesture. "I don't know what to do," his voice sounded vulnerable.

Mary walked to him and lightly grasped his upper arms. "You've already done the hardest part. You agreed to try to establish a connection with another person. Something tells me this took tremendous courage. Now we just let things grow as they will. No pressure. No demands. No expectations you have to meet."

Adam looked into Mary's eyes for s brief instant, then nodded. She let go and stepped aside. "I keep taking up your time, and Elena is going to start charging me for it. Best be at it."

He gave her one more quick look and then swiftly strode toward the laundry room.

★★★★★

Soosie was still chatting with Emily just outside the kitchen door. Turning into the laundry, Adam saw Myron fidgeting with his caddy. He looked up sharply. Adam rewarded him with a slight twitch of the corner of his mouth.

"That was almost a smile," Myron said.

"Yeah. Whatever."

During the teens' time at the center, it was customary for Olivia or Lidiya to walk the couple of blocks to the drug store and the post office while the residents were breakfasting. Elena would use the same time to work on the computer or do other business-related jobs. Today, it looked like Elena was going through the mail, which had stacked up in her absence, when Soosie pushed the vacuum cleaner through the main room. Soosie continued down the hall and turned into Emily's room as her cleaning first stop.

She had just finished vacuuming Emily's and Mary's rooms when Olivia came through the front door bearing a large bag from the pharmacy in one hand and a stack of mail in the other.

Soosie pushed the vacuum cleaner into the empty room because it was a quick clean compared to Bert's room next door with its tchotchkes, endless ruffles, and rhinestones blinging everything.

As she maneuvered the vacuum and her caddy out of the empty room, she glanced up. Through the open office door, she saw Olivia hovering over and patting Elena's shoulder. Elena had her head in her hands. It was obvious something was wrong.

Soosie was tempted to find an excuse that would let her get closer to see if she could find out what was happening, but it wasn't any of her business, so she headed in to tackle Bert's room. She had actually forgotten about what she had observed until midafternoon when Olivia came into the laundry room, where all three teens were folding clothes. Olivia's smile was in place as always, but it looked forced.

"Elena wants you to know she understands that this place has really been taking advantage of your willingness to jump in whenever you're asked. This wasn't what you were hired for, but you three have been lifesavers this last couple of weeks. So I just want to warn you, we're gonna continue to abuse you the next couple of days while Elena is out for Arturo's surgery, which is scheduled for Wednesday."

All three nodded their assent.

Olivia opened her mouth as though she wanted to say something further but closed it with a little shake of her head. She looked tired and sad when she headed back out the door.

It was so unlike her bubbly Southern personality. The three teens exchanged concerned glances. Although nothing had been said, they felt instinctively something more than Arturo's surgery was weighing on Olivia.

Alma came in the door before they could return to finishing their day's work. She, too, wore a look of concern on her face.

She remembered to paste on a smile just as she placed three plastic baggies on the folding table. "Fresh strawberry muffins." She sighed. "And I'm off to still another baseball game. See you tomorrow," and she was out the door as well.

When the three headed up front to check out, they saw David, Steve, and Emily sitting at the table and drinking coffee. They looked like the teenagers felt—vaguely unsettled.

Adam had just slid his ID badge through the time clock when Myron touched his shoulder and tipped his head in the direction of the hall.

Adam saw Mary standing outside her door. She smiled and waved goodbye. Adam spontaneously returned both gestures before heading out the door. Myron gave Mary a thumbs-up and followed.

Although Adam just silently stared out the bus window on the trip back to the Pitt, Myron sensed a flicker of light in him. Myron offered up a silent prayer that life wouldn't screw things up for his roommate this time.

✶✶✶✶✶

The next day, everyone noticed something was continuing to bother Olivia and Lidiya. Both seemed preoccupied and unusually quiet as they went about their duties. Olivia didn't even indulge in chitchat with Bert when she brought her to the table for breakfast. Lidiya was generally quiet but always flashed a warm smile and acknowledged people with a cheery tone. Today she was just quiet.

Midmorning, Steve cornered Myron in the room he shared with Clarence. "You kids have any idea of what the hell is going

124

on around here? Something is eating the girls bad, but they're all clammed up."

Myron shook his head. "No, sir. No one has said anything to us."

"You three are all over this place. You overhear anything?"

Again Myron shook his head. "Actually, there hasn't been anything to hear."

"Well, I wish somebody would just come out and tell us if something bad is incoming so we can dive for the nearest bunker. All this secretive stuff is just getting on everyone's nerves," he said, shaking his head as he swung out the door.

As the day wore on, the air almost crackled with the tension. Olivia and Lidiya looked more and more hunted as they passed back and forth under the intense gaze of the residents. Even the three teens were beginning to feel jumpy in this atmosphere. It actually came as a relief when Alma handed out her usual end-of-day snack and it was time to clock out.

Mary and Emily had both just stepped out of Emily's room and were heading toward the dining room table where the other residents were gathered. As they passed the kids, Mary reached out to lightly squeeze Adam's arm and give him one of her warm smiles, which belied the strain in her face.

Instead of heading to the table with Mary, Emily followed the trio out of the center. "Olivia claims tonight's *Sentinel* wasn't delivered. We're guessing it has been stashed to keep us from reading it, so I'm just going to buy a copy at the drugstore. See you tomorrow."

✶ ✶ ✶ ✶ ✶

Jarett came out of the office when the kids burst through the Pitt door, but he didn't need to call out to them. They were already bearing down on him.

"How'd you know there was another letter in the paper?" he asked.

"Because the ladies at the care center were claiming it wasn't delivered so the old people couldn't see it," Adam said.

"Good for them, because it isn't pretty."

After following Jarett into the office, all three teens sat on the couch at the same time, with Soosie hunkered down between Myron and Adam. They collectively leaned forward.

"Okay, some of this is going to be hard to hear."

He shook the paper and began reading.

To the Editor:

Despite the multiple complaints I have filed with the state on behalf of the residents trapped in the substandard and unsafe Soda Springs Care Center, I have been unable to convince them to conduct an inspection—until recently. I was able to provide proof the center is employing three teens who are currently incarcerated by the State of Oregon for various criminal activities.

My investigations into these three indicate one is a member of Soda Springs' most notorious criminal family. We can only wonder how much personal property has gone missing from these poor people since he has had access to their rooms.

Myron looked away and bit his lip. After a moment, Jarett continued.

The second person employed is a female who was in court within the last year on the charge of aggravated assault against a family member. How desperate is a facility that it would employ a person convicted of violence to interact with the elderly?

Although Myron and Adam flinched away, expecting Soosie to erupt from the couch, she inexplicably burst into tears instead. Jarett grabbed a couple of tissues from the box on his desk and held them out.

Myron reached out to take them and pushed them into Soosie's hands. She abruptly turned her face into his shoulder. Myron automatically wrapped his arm around her. Just as abruptly, Soosie fought out of his light hold, flinging his arm away from her. She pushed off the couch and went to sit in the easy chair.

Jarett watched. "You okay, Soosie?"

Flushing, she nodded, keeping her eyes averted from the couch. Jarett continued.

The third teenager has been in state custody for a number of years, indicating issues prohibiting his placement in another living situation, such as a foster home. Yet again, this unstable individual has access to the vulnerable population housed in the Soda Springs Care Center.

Myron glanced at Adam. He was rigid, and his expression was frozen.

As a result of my investigations into the various unsavory and unsafe conditions at Soda Springs Care Center, the state has agreed to do a full investigation into both the facility and the circumstances that allow the residents to be jeopardized by the owners, the management, and the staff.

Jarett folded the paper. "I just want you to know that as soon as we saw this, Dustin went roaring down to the newspaper. According to the editor, this letter was never supposed to be published. He doesn't know how it ended up in the paper. He said he was going to conduct an investigation to see if it was just one of those accidents that happen at deadline or if somehow Adah manipulated one of her former coworkers into sneaking it in. If that is the case, then somebody will be looking for work by morning. He also promised to put a full retraction in the online edition immediately and also see that the retraction is on the first page in next week's paper. He swore the next time Adah Skelton's name appears in the *Sentinel*, it will be over her obituary."

A few silent moments passed before Jarett spoke again. "I'm sorry, guys. I don't have a choice anymore. I have to pull you out. Before, it didn't directly affect you; this time, you were targeted. I want you to get your scrubs washed and packed. I'll contact Mrs. Fuentes tomorrow."

While Adam and Soosie sat slumped, Myron leaned forward. "Sir, Mrs. Fuentes won't be there tomorrow. Her husband is having back surgery. It also means if we aren't there, Olivia and Lidiya will have to try to handle everything alone, including the cleaning and the laundry. I would like permission to go in anyway.

"What was in the paper about me is what I have been hearing my whole life. My name alone is enough for people to automatically assume I'm up to no good. I guess I'm kinda used to it. But, even knowing my name, Mrs. Fuentes was willing to give me a chance, and I would hate to bail on her when she really needs the help now."

He and Jarett stared at each other for a long moment.

"You have a point," Jarett said at last. "Mrs. Fuentes welcomed you three without reservation or judgment. I suspect she would totally understand if we yanked you, but leaving her in the lurch isn't exactly the way we would like to end things either." Jarett tapped the newspaper against his knee as he mulled the situation. "Okay, you can go back tomorrow, Myron."

*****

When Dustin came to shut off the door alarm in the morning, he was surprised to see all three teens waiting.

"I thought just Myron was going in today."

"He made so much noise getting ready this morning, he woke me up. Since I was already awake…" Adam's voice trailed off.

Soosie fixed her eyes on Dustin. "Really, you would let these two loose without someone responsible in charge?"

Dustin held up his hands. "Let me grab the other passes."

When they got off the bus in front of the care center, the threesome saw David sitting on the porch. He raised his cigar-holding hand in greeting as they crossed the street and mounted the steps.

"Just wanted you kids to know we've hired a hit on the witch. A couple of gallons of water and a bag of balloons are being delivered later. She even looks in your direction and we're going to melt her." He took a puff on his cigar. "Glad she didn't scare you off."

After clocking in, the teens headed toward the laundry room. Olivia was just coming out the door carrying one of the cleaning caddies when she spotted the kids and stopped.

"Dayammm," she said. "You kids have some real grit. Most folks would be grabbing the last train out of town after all those whoppers Adah put in the paper."

Myron reached out to take the caddy from her. "For some of us, it's nothing new," he said.

"Y'all also probably saw the state's gonna be doing an inspection of this place. Lidiya and I knew before the paper came out because Elena got a letter about it."

The memory of Elena with her head in her hands popped into Soosie's head. "That was Monday, wasn't it? I saw her when I was cleaning up front. She looked pretty upset."

"She sure was, sugar. Her having to worry and deal with Arturo's surgery and the state wanting to come waltzing in here to do their inspection. It's just more than one body can handle."

"What do they do during an inspection?" Myron asked.

"Oh, normally they just poke around looking for obvious safety issues, how clean the place is, if the medication records are up to date, stuff like that. But when they are coming cuz of a complaint, they can get right ruthless and use any little thing as an excuse to yank the license and shut this place down. It's just gonna depend on how bad Adah lied on us in the stuff she filed and how cantankerous the inspector is."

Lidiya leaned out from Steve and Clarence's door. "Olivia, Clarence is ready. Once we get him to the table, I'll come help you with Bert." Her face lit up when she saw the teens. "Oh, somebody is about to have a good day after all. Don't go away, please."

Olivia trotted in Lidiya's direction and disappeared from view. A couple of minutes later, Lidiya pushed Clarence's chair through the door. He was staring at the blanket covering him. When she was within a few feet of the trio, Steve swung out of the room. As soon as he saw them, he burst into a chorus of the Beatles' "Good Day, Sunshine."

Clarence looked up startled. Immediately his face contorted into the expression the three had learned was a smile. He waved his arm and began jabbering sounds.

Impulsively, Soosie stepped over and gave Clarence a hug and a kiss on his cheek. He pounded his arm on the chair in delight.

"He's gonna dine out on that for a whole year," Steve said as he shook both Myron and Adam's hands. "Kids, you have balls. Everyone was figuring yesterday was the last day we would see you. We kinda assumed your facility wouldn't keep putting you in the line of fire by letting you continue to work here, let alone you being willing to be moving targets for the bitch sniper."

Myron handed the caddy to Soosie. "I'll take Clarence up front, Lidiya."

"And if we don't get Bert to the table, she's gonna start eating her blankets," Olivia said as she headed up the hall with Lidiya stepping from behind the chair and following. They disappeared around the corner into the front wing.

The trolley bearing the breakfast trays trundled out of the kitchen pushed by Alma. She looked startled to see Adam and Soosie. "Myron here, too?" she asked.

Soosie nodded. "He just took Clarence up to the table."

Her broad face broke into a huge smile. "If I wasn't so fat, I'd just break into my happy dance right now. Adam, would you mind?" she asked.

Adam took the handle of the trolley and pushed it toward the dining room.

As he came into view, Emily got up from the table and headed down the hall to Mary's door. In a moment she returned with Mary.

Adam had just set the first tray in front of David when Mary swept him into a hug. Although he raised his arms, he didn't actually return the embrace. When she let go and stepped back, the yearning for contact was clear in his eyes, but his expression was neutral.

"I was afraid I wouldn't see you again," she said softly to him.

"Yeah, me too," he admitted in a whisper, looking away from her.

She smiled comfortingly and lightly squeezed his hand before going to sit down by Emily.

Adam resumed distributing the trays and then headed back to the laundry room.

Back in the laundry, Soosie was shaking out cleaning cloths and shoving them into her caddy. She looked up as Adam came into the room to get his caddy. Myron was filling a mop bucket in the sink.

"I hope you guys know I'm feeling like a total fraud here," Soosie began. "We're here today, but what about tomorrow when they find out we really aren't going to be sticking around?"

Myron and Adam both looked troubled as they nodded. "Well, maybe we can figure out some way to make it happen again," Myron said as he steered the bucket out the door with the mop handle.

The day became more and more difficult for the three to handle as the various residents continued to express their appreciation for the young peoples' willingness to show up. It didn't improve their discomfort when Olivia let everyone know Arturo's surgery had been seemingly successful and Elena should be back on Thursday.

By the time Alma brought each of them a cinnamon roll in Styrofoam containers, they were all looking thoroughly haunted.

As they made their way out the door, they answered all the various farewells only with noncommittal waves.

Chapter 23

When the three teens pushed through the door at the Pitt, Jarett came out of the common room. "Someone here to see you, Myron."

It was so rare there were any visitors to the Pitt, Adam and Soosie stopped as well.

A beautiful young woman rushed out of the common room and threw herself into Myron's arms.

Myron swooped her up and spun her around. "Viv." He set her down, grabbed her hand, and held on with his eyes locked on her face.

She reached out and slid her fingers along his jaw line. "You are so handsome, kid."

Jarett cleared his throat. "You can use the office to talk, Myron."

Looking over the young woman's head, Myron smiled his appreciation and then turned toward the office. He didn't let go of her hand as he pulled her along. He closed the door.

Jarett and Adam exchanged looks. They were positively drooling. Soosie shook her head in disgust. She stomped up to her room.

She almost tore her scrub top, ripping it off over her head. She flung it in the corner of her room before kicking out of the scrub pants. Sliding into jeans and a tee-shirt, she threw herself on her bed, viciously jamming the pillow under her head.

She was flaming pissed. Myron had never let on he had a girl-friend, let alone one freakin' Barbie-doll perfect, right down to her flippy little sundress and pale-plum pedicure.

Handsome. She had called him handsome. Thick brown hair, velvety brown eyes, and square jaw. Big deal. Was the chick so dumb she didn't know he was a Tatum? And Jarett was let-ting them use his office for what—to talk? A make-out session was more like it. She could just picture them crawling all over each other.

She suddenly launched herself off her bed and headed for the stairs. She sat down where she had a clear view of the front part of the first floor.

Surprisingly, the door to the office opened just as she sat down. The young woman was still picture perfect, from lipstick to hair. Myron didn't have a hot-and-bothered flush to him either.

He draped his arm over her shoulders and she wrapped her arm around his waist as he walked with her to the door. They let go of each other when he opened the door. She gave him an-other hug and a kiss on his cheek before floating out the door. He watched for a moment, then lifted his hand in farewell.

After closing the front door, he looked into the common room before turning towards the stairs. Soosie knew that was her cue to slip back upstairs before he saw her, but perverseness kept her butt firmly planted on the step. She continued to stare at him as he climbed up toward his room.

Catching sight of her, his unexpected expression propelled her off the stair tread and flying back up the stairs.

* * * * *

"You didn't tell me you had a girlfriend," Adam said as he watched Myron wrestle the scrub shirt over his head.

Emerging, Myron looked at him in surprise. "Dude, Vivienne is my cousin."

"Cousin? Really? Can I have her phone number then?"

"I'll have to check with her husband."

"Husband? You're kidding."

"No. She and Trevor got married after they graduated from college. That's been three or four years now."

"So how come the sudden visit?"

"Family business."

"Don't take this the wrong way, but with your family that sounds kinda like a *Godfather* thing."

Myron sat down on his bed to put his shoes back on. "Actually, it really is about family, as in kith and kin, as Grandma Weaver says. And no, I'm not going to tell you what it is, because then I would have to kill you."

"So it is a *Godfather* thing."

"I'm going to go talk to Jarett about tomorrow," Myron said standing up and exiting the room.

Jarett came into the dining area later. "Okay, you three are cleared to work one more day. I called to make an appointment with Elena, but the swing shift staff said she has let them know she won't be in until Friday. Apparently there are issues related to her husband's surgery that haven't resolved to the satisfaction of his surgeon, so she wants to stay close."

"And Myron, I have a question for you. Do you have any more cousins in your family like the one who showed up today? If so, phone numbers would be appreciated."

Myron grinned. "Right now the family tree is pretty picked

over as far as eligible female relatives. But if you're willing to wait about fifteen years or so, there are a few coming up who aren't spoken for yet."

"I'll get back to you on that."

Soosie pushed away from the table and picked up her dishes. Something inside of her had taken a little leap at the news that Barbie was actually related to Myron. But something else was pricking at her brain.

She climbed back towards her room. Just as her foot landed on the tread where she had sat earlier, she made the connection. It was the look on Myron's face when he had seen her sitting there. It had been cool. Not cold, but without the warmer looks of concern and the awareness he usually wore when he looked at her. It was…she struggled to find the word. *Detached.* That was it. It was like she no longer was of any concern to him. She was surprised to find how much that thought hurt and immediately was angry because it did hurt.

She felt the need to do something, so she gathered the scrubs she had slung off earlier, as well as a few other items needing washing. She carried everything to the basement, where she stuffed them in the washer.

Instead of heading back to her room like she usually did while her clothes were in the washer, she sat down in an old blue plastic chair. It rocked under her weight, and she shifted to the tan folding chair, fixing her gaze on the washing machine. Her thoughts were cascading like the water in the machine.

Only one more day, and she wouldn't be dealing with Bert's muumuus or Paul's delicates anymore. It also meant she wouldn't be hanging in the laundry room at the center with Myron and Adam.

Not that they interacted a lot. Adam and Myron were mostly quiet while they worked, but they were there, and she had somehow come to rely on their presence in her days. True, Adam didn't acknowledge her existence often, but he still was willing to step up when she was confronted by some mechanical or technical problem, like the time one of Steve's tee-shirts had somehow gotten itself wrapped up under the agitator. She had been afraid she was going to have to tear it to get it out, but Adam had taken the agitator apart, saving the shirt.

And Myron, who had quietly taken all the punches she had thrown at him, literally and verbally. He had shielded her, even from her own dumbass actions, never asking for or even apparently expecting any kind of reciprocation.

And now it was all changing again, and she was freakin' done with change! From the time her father had slipped on the ice and injured his brain on his flat-out landing, she felt like every day had been a crazed ride on the rollercoaster from hell.

She was tired of constantly being coiled tight into self-protectiveness, constantly being vigilant to be sure she could strike first at anything and everything.

She was tired of life's mirages floating here and there, whispering, "It's going to be okay," because it never was.

And when Sammy had been sucked away into the system, her careful plans vaporized, and she was left with a future full of…nothing to grab onto.

It was as if she had been so focused on just trying to stay afloat through everything that she had lost who she was, who she wanted to be, what she wanted.

Her emotions began to spin in time with the washing machine. Burying her face in her hands, she gave vent to the storm within her.

* * * * *

After turning off the lights in their room, Adam lay with his arms folded behind his head. Tomorrow was it. They would go in, do what they always did, and then at the end of the day, they would clock out, get on the bus, and never go back. The connection he had with Mary was going to be snapped. He wasn't surprised. It had always felt insubstantial, like something that couldn't and wouldn't last. But what surprised him was his feeling of loss. He had tried to be so careful to give the appearance he was engaging with Mary without actually committing any emotion to it. But an unacknowledged hunger had begun to grow when she had given him a squeeze, a touch, the recognition that he existed and that somehow he was important to her.

He wrestled with the idea of trying to say goodbye before they left tomorrow, but the words simply wouldn't coalesce in his brain. In the end, he decided to just walk out the door with Myron and Soosie and not look back. Maybe if you didn't say goodbye, you could pretend it hadn't mattered.

Chapter 24

The first sign something was not right the next day was the absence of David from his usual smoking place. David had always been there when they got off the bus. Even on chilly and wet days, he'd be bundled up while smoking his cigar.

The three looked at each other with concern etched in their eyes. They hurried through clocking in then hustled toward the laundry room, slowing as they passed David's room. From behind the closed door, they could hear the rumble of quiet voices.

Buoyed by relief, they continued on. Steve swung out of his room. "Morning, kids," he said. "If Clarence starts fussing, will you let him know I'm on a recon mission and will report back in due time?"

"Will do, sir," Myron said.

Then, stealthily looking up and down the hall, even though there was no one else there, Steve knocked a quick code on David's door. The door opened, and the kids saw Paul's face peer around it as Steve quickly crutched through.

Myron and Adam looked at each other. "Okay, that was weird," Adam said.

They had barely switched on the lights in the laundry room when Olivia arrived. She looked totally frazzled.

"Lawd a mercy, kids. This place is gonna be the death of me. I'm going to be taking to one of those empty beds, and y'all are gonna have to wait on me. If it ain't one thing, it is two others. Right now, I am deputizing all three of you as nursing assistants for today, and the cleaning and laundry will just have to hang."

"Okay," Myron said uncertainly as he exchanged looks with the other two.

"So, just when you think it can't get worse, here's what happens: they ended up taking Arturo back to surgery last night because a blood clot had formed in the first surgical site and was pressing on nerves. According to Elena, they were able to clean it out, but they have him on a special watch to make sure it doesn't happen again. She's staying close until the all-clear is raised.

"Then, at three this morning, Lidiya gets a call from her son-in-law telling her her daughter is going into labor two months early and they were being sent up to the Oregon Health & Science University just in case. So, of course, Lidiya lit out of here as fast as she could. And all that means that it's just us four to keep this place going."

The three teens nodded cautiously.

"Soosie, if you can help me get Miss Bert up to the table, then we can get Tilly and Katie bathed, changed, and fed. Myron, can you do Clarence? He'll need to be sponge bathed, including the dangly bits, put in a new diaper, and then dressed in the light pajama bottoms and tee-shirt before he gets in his chair and up to the table. Don't forget his slippers and lap robe.

"Adam, can you help Alma get the trays loaded and take the trolley up front for everyone else? Just leave Tilly's and Katie's in the kitchen. Soosie and I will come get them."

She spun on her heel and headed back toward the front. After a moment's hesitation, Soosie followed.

Myron turned toward Clarence's room while Adam went into the kitchen.

It was an awkward hour as the three attempted to follow Olivia's instructions with varying degrees of success. Finally, though, Bert and Clarence were at the table, along with Emily and Mary. Missing were David, Paul, and Steve.

Clarence babbled his sounds as he waved his arm at Steve's chair. Myron looked at Emily and Mary.

"We haven't seen any of those three, and that does not bode well. They are up to something," Emily said.

Myron headed to the back room where Soosie and Olivia were. He noted David's door was still closed as he passed. He stopped in the doorway of the back room, carefully keeping his gaze on the floor. "Olivia?"

"We're all good here," she said cheerfully.

Myron looked up and saw Soosie standing by Tilly's bed, carefully spooning food into her mouth.

"Steve, David, and Paul haven't shown for breakfast. Should I go ahead and feed Clarence?"

Olivia dropped the spoon she was using to feed Katie back into the bowl. "Those danged old reprobates. I do not need them acting out today." She zipped out of the room and up the hall with Myron on her heels.

She began pounding on David's door. "You three turn off the porn and get to the breakfast table. This is not the day for you to be getting on my last nerve."

The door swung open. Paul stood there in pink pedal pushers and a flowered blouse, with the lacy tops of pink anklets

143

carefully folded above the tops of his black athletic shoes. "We are not watching porn. We were having an important meeting." He then huffily stumped his walker toward the dining room with Steve following. David scrambled some papers into the drawer of the computer desk in his room before rolling along with the other two.

Olivia stood with her arms akimbo until they disappeared around the corner into the dining room.

*****

After the breakfast trays had been gathered and returned to the kitchen, the three teens gathered back in the laundry room. Olivia stopped at the doorway with a glass of sweet tea in her hand. "Come join me in the dining room, and let's figure out how we're gonna get through the rest of the day."

After a division of responsibility was made between the four of them, the teens alternated between helping Olivia, caring for the residents, and doing the laundry. Soosie helped Olivia feed Tilly and Katie while Adam and Myron had lunch with the residents.

Soosie and Olivia arrived with their lunch trays as Adam began to clear the others. Myron pushed Clarence back to his room with Steve following.

As Myron lifted Clarence and settled him for his afternoon nap, Steve commented, "Clarence trusts you. When he doesn't like somebody, he gets just as rigid as an old board when they try to put him to bed. I trust you too," he finished enigmatically as he swung over to sit in Clarence's just-vacated chair. "Close the door, Myron."

Myron did as he was asked then looked back at Steve, his eyebrow raised quizzically.

"Take a load off." Steve pointed to the other recliner in the room.

Myron sat on the edge, keeping his eyes on the older man.

Steve leaned forward. "Okay. I'm going to make a wild guess here that as a Tatum, you are well-schooled in keeping your mouth shut about a lot of things. Right?"

Myron nodded warily.

"It's why we have decided to provide you with certain information." Steve paused and looked around like he was expecting to find the National Security Agency in their midst. He resumed. "Now, it is possible before this night is over, a coup may take place in which a downtrodden population is being jacked around by a governmental agency and threatened with the loss of their home to satisfy an evil entity who has too long wandered unfettered in the streets of Soda Springs.

"Affiliated with this besieged facility are people who have proven their mettle in the current firefight. However, if and when the coup occurs, access will be denied to all who are not actual residents on the morrow."

Myron's gaze held steady with Steve's for a long moment. "I will let Adam and Soosie know when we get back to the Pitt we can sleep in tomorrow."

Steve grinned and threw up his two fingered salute. "Peace, brother."

David was waiting in the hall when Myron left the room. In answer to David's gaze, Myron nodded slightly. David stuck his unlit cigar in his mouth, wheeled around, and motored in the direction of the front porch.

When Myron returned to the laundry room, he automatically began folding the towels Adam had piled on the table. Deep in thought, he didn't seem to be aware of his actions or of the other two occupants.

When he heard a door close in the hall, he abruptly left the laundry room and walked down the hall. He lightly tapped on David's door.

It was Steve's face peering out when the door was cracked. Seeing Myron, he opened the door and motioned him in.

Myron waited until the door was shut behind him. "How are you going to manage everything if it's just you here?"

David looked at him. "We'll manage. After all, we didn't get to be this old and infirm by not managing. We're taking a stand, son. And when you do that, you got to be willing to pay whatever price is necessary." He gestured toward Steve's empty pantleg. "It's a lesson our generation learned well."

✶ ✶ ✶ ✶ ✶

Adam was just coming out of the laundry room with an armload of towels when Myron returned.

"For the back ward?" Myron asked. "I'll take them." He hefted them out of Adam's arm and strode purposefully down the hall.

When Myron returned to the laundry room, he began rooting through the maintenance cupboard. After shifting a couple of things around, he closed the door without taking anything out.

Soosie and Adam exchanged quizzical looks before she gathered up Emily's clothes and headed out the door. Adam pushed the front hall's large hamper in her wake.

As soon as he was alone, Myron went back to the maintenance closet and pulled a couple of items out. He measured a length of twine from a roll and cut it with the utility scissors. Then he tore off a strip of duct tape. He grabbed the other large hamper and pushed it out the door toward the back room.

With a lifetime of family experience behind him, it only took a few minutes for him to accomplish his mission. As he left the back room, Steve motioned to him. "Mind getting Clarence up?"

Myron changed Clarence and redressed him before placing him back in his chair. Clarence jabbered his sounds at him as Myron made sure his feet were comfortably positioned and tucked the robe around him.

Steve translated. "Clarence is saying he is proud to have known you. You're a good soldier."

Myron shook Clarence's hand. "I'm glad to have known you too, sir." He glanced questioningly at Steve.

Steve grinned. "We'll be fine, kid." He let go of the crutch handle and held out his hand. "And I'm like Clarence. Proud to call you friend."

When it was time for the kids to clock out, Adam looked down the hall toward Mary's room. Olivia was in the office making notes on the computer. "Mary and Emily went to get some things from the drugstore," she said tiredly. "You kids were just a lifesaver today. Unfortunately, tomorrow's gonna be hell on wheels."

Myron looked at her sharply.

Chapter 25

Jarett was once again waiting for them when they came through the door of Pittison House. "Today we got an email message advising us not to allow you to return to the center. Quote, for their own protection, end quote.

"I want you to wash your scrubs and pack them up. You three are officially through. We'll see if we can find you some other positions to fill the next few months until you're collectively out of here."

Soosie and Adam looked at Myron, expecting him to enter some type of argument about being needed at the center because of both Elena's and Lidiya's absences. Instead, he remained silent as he stared straight ahead.

"I'll take everything over tomorrow and talk with Mrs. Fuentes myself. And if any of you have someplace you would like to work—fast food, gas station, etc. —let me know, and we'll see what we can do. Make sure I have your stuff first thing in the morning." He waved his hand in dismissal.

Myron led as the trio climbed the stairs. Inside their room, Myron changed clothes disjointedly while Adam ducked his flailing arms by hunkering on his bed.

"Okay, that was intense—and life-threatening," Adam said as he stood up.

Myron mumbled a distracted "Sorry."

Adam had felt Myron was hiding something ever since mid-afternoon, when Myron returned to the laundry room. Now Adam thought it might be connected to the email message Jarett had gotten. He decided to push a little. "So I wonder who sent the email? And why? Elena wouldn't ask us to stay away. Neither would Olivia or Lidiya. Suppose it was the crazy newspaper lady?"

Myron shook his head. "I think it came from friends."

"Friends? Dude, in case you don't remember, we're both kinda short of people who fit that description."

"No. We actually do have some friends—now." Myron stared steadily at Adam.

Adam stared back. Then he made the connection. "The people at the care center," he said.

"Boom."

"Why would they do—" Adam stopped. "Something is going on, and you know what it is, don't you."

"Possible."

"You going to tell me?"

The dinner buzzer sounded. "Later. Maybe."

★★★★★

At dinner, Myron just picked at his food, leaving more on his plate than he ate. Adam kept directing puzzled glances at him. From across the table, Soosie recognized that whatever had been bugging Myron this afternoon was still eating at him, and he obviously hadn't shared it with Adam.

Myron gave up his pretense of eating and took his plate to the kitchen before heading back upstairs.

Adam and Soosie were just finishing when Myron came back downstairs with an armload of both his and Adam's scrubs. He didn't say a word to anyone as he headed to the basement.

After rinsing and putting his dishes in the dishwasher, Adam headed to the basement as well.

The washer was already filling when Adam stepped off the stairs. Myron was seated in the folding chair. Adam sat down next to him but said nothing.

After the silence had stretched for several minutes, Adam spoke. "My people skills definitely suck, but I'm here if you need to, like, talk or anything. It's kinda what friends are for."

Myron turned his head and shot a quick half-smile to his roommate. "You still gonna be my friend when I show I'm a real Tatum?"

"You planning on robbing a bank?"

"I think I may have to go AWOL."

"You mean run? That is pretty serious shit, man. You'll get bounced out of here in a heartbeat, not to mention blow your whole 'good guy' thing forever. Why would you even think about it?"

Myron hung his head, letting his inner distress show for the first time. "Because if I don't, some good people might unintentionally be getting themselves in deep trouble."

Adam shook his head in confusion. "Dude, I have no idea what you're talking about."

"Look, you have to pinky swear you won't tell a single person what I'm going to tell you, okay? I was kinda sworn to secrecy."

Adam held up his hand and Myron hooked his pinkie finger over Adam's. "Okay. Done."

"The people at the care center are planning some kind of takeover to prevent the state from getting in for the inspection and forcing them out. Steve told me that by tomorrow morning, the only people allowed in the facility would be those who already lived inside. No one else—apparently not even Olivia and Lidiya."

"So?"

"Come on, man. They can't take care of themselves. Who's gonna get Clarence up or take care of Tilly and Katie? If they don't let Alma in, who's gonna cook? Who's gonna make sure they get their medications?"

"Okay, I see where you're going. But even if you pull a runner, what makes you think they're going to let you in?"

"I may not do what my family does, but it doesn't mean I can't."

"So we're going to add breaking and entering to our resume as well?" Adam asked.

"Not ours. Mine."

"Sorry, man, but I have to go with you."

"Why? You think the room mothers are gonna blame you for me taking off?"

"Ah, no. But without me, you're never going to be able to get out of this place without setting off the alarm."

"You know the code?"

"Nope, but I do know how to disable it. Used to do it a lot when I needed to get a break from whatever creeper they assigned to be my roommate," Adam said. "So without me your plan isn't going to happen. That means I'm in."

"Me too."

Both young men jumped at the unexpected voice. Spinning around in their chairs, they saw Soosie sitting on the stairs.

"How long have you been there?" Adam asked.

She stood up and finished descending to the basement floor. "Long enough to know I'm coming with you."

Myron protested. "Soosie, things are going to get really un-cool at some point. You don't—"

"What? Want to be thrown in juvie jail? Been there, done that. I'm coming and you don't have a choice, so don't waste your breath."

"And we don't have a choice why?" Adam asked.

"Because I'll rat you out otherwise."

Chapter 26

Soosie was waiting outside the door when Myron and Adam opened it. She was holding a plastic bag with the extra changes of clothes and overnight items they had decided they might need. Myron motioned her into the room. Taking her bag, he stuffed it inside his blue duffle along with his and Adam's stuff.

As she watched him, she realized his bed was actually made, while Adam's looked like it had never been made in the entire time he had lived at the Pitt.

Hefting the bag, Myron turned to look at the other two. His face was pale but determined. "Let's do this," he said.

They quietly crept down the stairs to the door. Adam pulled a tiny pocket knife out of his scrubs pocket and flipped open the blade. Slipping it under a small notch at the bottom of the house alarm, he gently popped off the cover. He reached back into his pocket for a tiny wad of paper, which he carefully placed between the two contacts. He then popped the cover back on.

"We're out of here," he whispered.

He unlocked and cracked the door. Then, motioning Myron and Soosie through, he followed and carefully shut it.

They tiptoed down the stairs and broke into a run once they hit the sidewalk. Myron led them around the corner of the block before pulling up. "Okay. I think we can slow it down." He was trembling.

"You okay?" Adam asked.

Myron shook his head. "I just blew up seventeen years of working really hard to be a good guy." He looked stricken.

"We can sneak back in if you want."

"No. It's done. Let's keep going."

They walked briskly after Myron reminded them they would look more suspicious if someone spotted them running.

It took them just over forty-five minutes to cover the three miles from the Pitt to the care center. When they reached the corner where they usually got off the bus, Adam and Soosie automatically crossed in the direction of the front door.

Myron hissed at them. "This way." He motioned them to follow him toward the alley at the back. He led them down to an opening between the cinder block wall of the care center's courtyard and the back wall of the neighboring hardware store.

"Up and over," he instructed as he reached up to set the blue duffle on top. Adam jumped and hoisted himself up the six-foot wall before scrambling over.

Myron interlaced his fingers and bent over so Soosie could step in his hand. He hoisted her until she was able to clamber on top of the wall as well before jumping up and swinging over himself.

Soosie and Adam looked at Myron questioningly. He swiftly crossed the court to the double door leading into the back ward. There he detached a length of twine taped to the outside door. Leaning in close to the door, he carefully tugged at it until there was a faint click as the deadbolt at the top of the door released. Grabbing the handle, he eased it open. Duct tape had kept the latch from being able to engage.

Putting his finger to his lips, he pointed in the direction of

Tilly and Katie. Adam and Soosie tiptoed through the ward, waiting by the back doors in the hall until Myron joined them.

"Okay, you're good," Adam whispered.

Myron shrugged. "Just basic Tatum stuff," he whispered back.

Turning in the direction of the laundry room, the teens noticed the doors to the men's rooms were already standing open and voices were coming from up front.

Adam tapped Myron on the shoulder and nodded his head in the direction of the back doors. A thick dowel that had been in the maintenance cupboard was now jammed through the doors handles.

Walking quietly, the trio headed up the hall. Soosie pointed at the kitchen, which was still dark. As they passed the laundry room, Adam stepped in to put the duffle on the folding table then followed his friends.

They peeked around the corner of the hall into the dining room. David's wheelchair was rolled up to the little table used by the employees. He was busily tapping away on his laptop. Wearing a military fatigue shirt over his tie-dyed tee-shirt, Steve watched. Paul was looking over David's shoulder while dressed in an old military fatigue shirt and jungle trousers with a boonie hat on his head.

Advancing around the corner into the main room, Myron raised his hand. "Hi, guys."

The three older men jumped. Paul grabbed something off the dining room table and swung it in their direction.

Myron threw his arms out, pushing Adam back and Soosie behind him. "Whoa," he said. "It's just us!"

Paul lowered his arm, waving the gun in his hand before tossing it on the table. "It's useless. Firing pin broke back about 1979.

And just what the hell are you three doing sneaking in here, anyway? We're old people. You could have given us a heart attack."

Oddly, Steve began to laugh and pound the table. He then held his hand out in David's direction. "I told you they would show up. You owe me a sawbuck."

The three teens exchanged bewildered glances.

Steve's eyes twinkled. "You seemed pretty concerned about us old people yesterday after I told you our plan. Then, when we were blocking the doors last night, I spotted your handiwork, Myron. Don't get me wrong, you did a damn good job of setting the door up to open without raising suspicion, but spotting trip wires was a skill those of us in country needed if we were gonna make it back."

"I trust they have been properly secured now?" Paul asked.

Myron pulled the twine and a wad of duct tape from his pocket and held them out. "Yes, sir."

David emphatically hit a key on his laptop. "And the first volley has officially been fired," he said as he backed his wheelchair out from the table. "Okay, kids. I guess you understand that now that you are in, you cannot leave until this is over."

All three nodded.

Just then the door behind David opened. Olivia stepped out, stopping when she saw the teens. "Hallelujah, brothers, my prayers are answered!" she whooped.

"Olivia?" Soosie said in surprise.

Olivia grinned at them. "There are two bed-sitting rooms upstairs, hunnybun. That's where Lidiya and I live."

David pulled his unlit cigar from his mouth and pointed it in the direction of the kids. "That's why we said we could manage. Olivia was part of the plan."

Olivia pushed past him. "Lidiya and I said we could probably manage, not me alone. And Lidiya is not going to be here for a while. They put her daughter on full bedrest, and somebody needs to stay with her."

Emily stalked into the dining area. "You said there would be coffee. There is no coffee yet."

Paul bristled. "Woman, we are at war. Some things just have to wait."

"We are not at war; we are staging a peaceful live-in."

Steve pulled himself up on his crutches. "Myron, let's go check on Clarence. A dove without her coffee can make a hawk look like a pet chicken."

"And Soosie and I will get Miss Bert up and at 'em," Olivia said.

Paul looked at Adam. "How much do you know about cooking, boy?"

Adam shook his head. "Other than PB&Js, nothing."

"Well, you're about to get a crash course, so come on. You turn on the lights," Paul said pointing to the kitchen. "I'll be right back."

When Paul returned, he was minus the boonie hat but wearing a red-and-yellow apron patterned in teapots and edged in yellow ruffles. He had a pink-flowered one with green ruffles slung over the crosspiece of his walker. He handed it to Adam. "Put it on, and then look over there in the cupboard to see if you can find the box of hair nets. Grab one for each of us. "

The acute embarrassment Adam felt putting on the apron and the hair net dissipated as he bounced around the kitchen grabbing whatever item Paul demanded while the man efficiently cooked mountains of scrambled eggs, pancakes, and turkey bacon.

Paul caught his amazed staring. "You know, kid, we all worked at something to fill up the years while we waited for our chance to get in this place. Me? I had my own diner. Cooked six days a week for almost forty years. Wanna bring that stack of plates over here?"

Paul swiftly filled each plate and handed it to Adam, who placed a cover over it, put in on a tray, and loaded the trolley. Under Paul's direction, he filled a couple of containers with syrup, added a plate of butter slices, and two carafes of coffee before pushing the trolley out the door and up the hall.

One tray remained on the trolley after Adam distributed them. David looked around. "Where's Myron?" he asked.

"I'll find him," Adam volunteered. He located Myron loading sheets into the large washer.

"Hey, breakfast is ready, and you're doing my job," Adam said.

"I just thought I would get a load going while Olivia and Soosie are feeding Tilly and Katie. And thanks, but I'm not really hungry."

"Come on, man, you barely ate anything last night. You need to eat something."

"No, really I'm good. I'm just not sure my stomach wants to handle food right now. Maybe later," Myron said as he shoved the hamper past Adam and out the door.

Adam went back to the dining room. David looked at him as he sat down. "He says he's not hungry."

"I've known a lot of teenage boys—thousands of them, in fact—and hungry is their middle name. If a boy isn't eating, then something is eating him."

Chapter 27

Olivia and Soosie had just arrived with their breakfast trays while Adam was wiping down the table and chairs. They sat at one of the big tables because David was continuing to use the smaller table as his "command center." Emily and Mary were also still at the table enjoying a leisurely second cup of coffee when someone rattled the front door. Its window was covered by kraft paper written with the words, "Hell no, we won't go!" so whoever was knocking appeared only as a vague outline.

David rolled over to the door. "We gave at the office," he called. "This is Chief Braden, and it is a violation of fire codes for these doors to be locked."

"Ben?" David said. "We can get out; you just can't get in. So it's okay."

"Mr. Hirsch? What in hell are you doing, sir?"
"Like I said in the email, we're taking a stand. We may be old, but we aren't stupid or senile, at least not yet. We don't want to be treated like slabs of meat that can be drop-kicked into any old place to suit Adah Skelton's latest blood hunt."

"I understand, but this is not the way to do it."

"This is exactly the way to do it. Nobody gets in until we have a guarantee somebody is going to give us a fair hearing."

"Ah, geez, the media is pulling up. Who all did you notify?"

David threw a grin in the direction of everyone at the table. "Every news outlet within a fifty-mile radius."

"You know, sooner or later, you're going to have to unlock the doors."

"Yeah, well, we'll let you know when that is."

David backed up his chair. "Steve go back to his room?" he asked the four women sitting at the table. Without waiting for an answer, he headed down the hall. Adam followed him with the food trolley.

Leaning forward, David pushed open the door and rolled partway into the room. Clarence's chair was reclined, and he was dozing in it. Steve was just exiting the bathroom.

"You mind taking over watching our email and Facebook page? There's someone I gotta talk to," David asked him.

"No problem."

David backed up and powered toward the laundry room. It was empty. He headed down the hall to the back ward. Again, there was nobody.

Puzzled, he reversed his chair and was just starting up the hall when Myron came out of the employee's bathroom.

David motioned to him. "Come with me, kid." He led Myron to his room, where David pivoted his wheelchair around. "Talk to me."

Myron turned his hands up in question. "About what?"

"It's been my experience that big strapping kids don't skip meals unless something is sticking in their craw. So spit it out."

Misery washed over Myron's face. "I kinda turned into my family today."

"How? You kids hold up the 7-Eleven on your way over?"

A ghost of a smile passed across Myron's face. "No, sir. It's just leaving the Pitt without permission is…"

"A bad thing. But I can think of a few thousand other things worse. Look, you did it because you were worried about us old-timers being able to take of ourselves, right?"

Myron nodded.

David reached for one of the cigars sitting on his computer table and stuck it in his mouth. "You know, there was this man, Jewish fellow, who lived a couple of millennia back. He said something like this: 'Greater love hath no man than this, that a man lay down his life for his friends.'" He looked at Myron. "One of the hardest things in life is doing something because you believe it's the right thing to do, especially when the doing requires personal sacrifice. It's what separates the men from boys. That's why you are a mensch in my book."

There was a light knock on the door, and Emily opened it. "They just announced we're on the early morning news right after the commercials!"

"Come on, Myron. This we gotta see."

Following David out the door, Myron turned toward Steve and Clarence's room. "I'll get Clarence if he's awake."

Everyone had just gotten to dining room when a wide shot of the care center appeared on the TV screen. Slowly the camera closed in until there was a close-up shot of the sign covering the front window. A voice said, "Today in downtown Soda Springs, a small town located about thirty-five miles south of Portland, a most unusual story is unfolding."

The camera shifted to the reporter. "Apparently at five thirty this morning, the residents of this care center took control of the building and have barred themselves inside in a protest against a state inspection. Although we have not yet been able to confirm the allegations, it appears the inspection was scheduled in response to a series of complaints filed by a local resident.

"In a statement issued by the residents, they assert they are happy in their living situation and the complaints filed with the state are retaliatory, based on a previous incident involving the complainant."

A heavily muscled man with a number of tattoos spilling out from under the sleeves of his black polo shirt passed behind the reporter, his shaved head and the earring in his ear gleaming in the morning sun. He stopped when he reached Chief Braden, who was leaning against a squad car in the background.

"Uh-oh," Adam said. "Dustin."

"Dustin?" Mary asked.

"One of the room mothers at the Pitt."

"He's in charge of you? He looks like somebody in uniform should be in charge of him," Paul commented.

"The room mothers are okay as you long as you sorta make an effort to stay on the right side of the rules," Adam said as the three teens exchanged uneasy looks.

"Let me see. It is probably not in the rules for residents to sneak out of the facility in the wee hours of the morning and lock themselves in with a bunch of old people who are also working the wrong side of the rules," Steve said while stroking his beard. "So what happens to you when this is over?"

"We'll be pulled out of the Pitt and stuck somewhere else, like detention or another place for more hardcore rule breakers," Soosie said.

"And you knew this when you left this morning?" Emily asked, stunned.

"You mean," Mary said, "you three put your own place to live in jeopardy to help make sure we had a chance of keeping our place?" She stared at each one of them, but her gaze lingered longest on Adam's face.

The three avoided looking at her.

David, who had continued to watch the television, reported. "Okay, the wicked witch has just landed her broom. Let's see if she is going to unleash the flying monkeys on us."

The kids leaned in to see a stout woman stalking in the direction of Chief Braden. She was dressed in a brown knit pantsuit and a voluminous gold satin blouse. Her brown hair defied the reality of the age in her face.

It was evident a confrontation was brewing when Adah stopped and engaged the chief. The reporter quickly moved to place the microphone in his hand near the two.

"Shouldn't you be doing something?" Adah snapped.

"What do you want me to do, Adah? Call in the SWAT teams and batter down the doors, fire tear gas through the windows, or maybe use flashbangs?"

"Well, anything would be more effective than you just standing around here holding your squad car up."

"SWAT's got better things to do than terrorize a bunch of seniors."

"What about the terror they have endured in being forced to live there? This place has been an abomination for decades, and it is time those poor people were rescued and put somewhere where they can get appropriate care."

At that moment, Elena stepped up next to the chief. "They are happy in their home. It is why they are doing this thing. You are the one who makes things bad for people."

"If it wasn't for me and my family, I would hate to think what a stink hole this town would be," Adah sneered.

The reporter turned back to the camera, fingering his earpiece. "I'm sorry, but I have just been advised we are going to cut away to regular programming at this time. However, stay tuned. We will be bringing you updates on this situation throughout the day." A commercial began.

"Are we going to let Elena in?" Emily asked.

David shook his head. "Can't. If we crack a door, they could rush this place before our demands are met. Nope, we are sitting tight."

Emily's expression was sour. "It doesn't feel right. It's her business."

"Exactly. And if they force all of us out of here, then she doesn't have a business anymore. If she were inside, Adah would allege she's behind all this. So we keep Elena out of it. It's the only way we can protect her."

Paul turned away, pointing his walker in the direction of the hall. "Come on, Adam. We got dishes to wash and lunch to plan. And maybe while we're doing that, these two nosy old biddies can spy on what's happening outside without being spotted."

"You know, Paul, your remark is totally sexist. Accurate, but sexist," Emily said as she got up. "Come on, Mary. Let's figure out how to watch them without them watching us."

*****

Soosie headed to the laundry room to get her cleaning caddy. Spotting Myron's blue duffle on the folding table, she remembered that she had stuffed Emily's books in along with her stuff. She dug them out before grabbing her caddy.

When she stopped in Emily's open doorway, she could see the older woman fidgeting with her vertical blinds. "Do you need help?" Soosie asked.

Emily smiled. "I'm just experimenting. I'm trying to figure out how I can look out without anyone seeing me or being able to look in."

Soosie held the books out. "I wanted to return these before," she paused, "before I get moved."

Emily left the window and sat down at her desk. "I'm curious, Soosie. Why you would risk coming here today knowing you're going to be punished for it?"

Soosie shrugged. "I guess because Myron and Adam were."

"Being loyal to your friends is a pretty good reason."

"Oh, they're not my friends. In fact, I hate Myron, and Adam is a real loser."

Tilting her head at the protest in Soosie's voice, Emily studied the girl. "If you really felt that way about the boys, it seems an odd choice to accompany them."

"Well…maybe. I don't know. It's…it's…" she stammered, desperately trying to avoid admitting she had become reliant on their presence.

"Complicated," Emily said. "A word that sums up much of life."

The noon news showed another shot of the care center while presenting an abbreviated story and promising full details and interviews in the evening news program. Mary and Emily reported that a few people were showing up to stare and point at the building before drifting away. The police chief had left, although there appeared to be more frequent drive-bys of the officers on duty. The only person maintaining constant surveillance was Adah, armed with her binoculars, reporter's notebook, and cell phone.

Adam was just pulling the door down on the dishwasher, which was loaded with the supper dishes, when Paul leaned around the kitchen door. "Hey, kid, you can finish the dishes later. The news is coming on."

Adam hit the start button. He untied his apron and tossed it onto the kitchen island as he headed out the door.

This time the reporter was standing in front of the care center. After summing up the situation, he identified Adah.

"Adah Skelton is the person who filed the original complaints with the state regarding alleged conditions she observed inside the Soda Springs Care Center. Ms. Skelton, could you please itemize your specific concerns for our viewers?"

"First of all, I would like viewers to know I have been a reporter for decades, so my powers of observation are quite excellent. Several months ago, I was repeatedly denied an opportunity to interview a woman who once stood at the forefront of education in Soda Springs. When I was finally able to enter the facility, I discovered this person was systematically being starved to the point of emaciation. Her condition was such she was no longer able to comprehend and answer my questions.

"As a result of my observation, I began to closely monitor the facility. During that time, I have observed that residents are allowed to smoke on the porch without consideration for the public who use the sidewalk. I have seen that poor dietary offerings are rampant by observing a resident who is grossly obese. Several residents are allowed to walk around the community without supervision, and they have employed juvenile delinquents currently incarcerated by the state to work with this very, very vulnerable population. One has to wonder what goes on when they are inside those walls."

The news reporter took over. "Yes. In an interesting coincidence, which may or may not be related to the situation at the care center, it has been reported all three teenagers who were previously employed are now missing from the residential group home in which they lived. It is unknown if they are, in fact, participating in the lock-out or if they simply took advantage of the situation to run.

"Finally, we were able to confirm with the Department of Human Services that an official will be inspecting the facility on Monday. We will be continuing to monitor the situation at the Soda Springs Care Center over the weekend," the news anchor concluded. "We now return you to the studio."

Steve held up the remote. "Anyone interested in getting their daily dose of depressing information, or should I shut it off?"

Various hands waved. "I'm good."

"Yeah, enough."

"Done."

After the television was shut off, Mary broke the silence. "Too bad Neva isn't around anymore. She'd snatch Adah's head right off and hand it to her."

"Who's Neva?" Steve asked.

David answered. "Neva was a local artist who lived by her own lights. These are some of the paintings she did," he said as he swept his arm in the direction of the abstracts covering the walls of the main room. "She had a huge heart and no tolerance for anyone who wielded their power against those not in a position to fight back. She and her husband owned this house for decades. Since they never had any children, Neva offered room and board to people, usually those who lived on very limited income, like Edith Marshfield, who was the librarian back when the whole library was located in a side room of city hall. Edith was truly a spinster librarian. Never married. Had no known family. Lived for her job. She finally got too old and frail to work anymore." David glanced at the three kids perched on the loveseat behind him. "Believe it or not, there was a time when you were done working, you pretty much got nothing. For Edith, what the city gave her was only a fraction of the pittance they had paid her when she was working. Neva kept a roof over Edith's head, food in her belly, clothes on her back, and medical care when she needed it. She maintained Edith's dignity by telling her the city was paying for it as part of her reward for her years of service. When Edith died, Neva paid for her funeral and made damn sure the city employees showed up to pay their respects.

"After Edith, Neva took in any elderly person who had no one and nothing. When her husband, Gerald, died, she sold the variety store they owned and used the money to turn this place into pretty much what you see today."

"How'd Elena end up with it?" Emily asked.

"Elena showed up here just a scared migrant kid who barely spoke English looking for a job. Neva and Gerald had loved traveling in Mexico, so Neva was pretty fluent in Spanish. She gave her a job in the laundry room, just like you kids. When Elena's family was ready to move onto the next crop, Neva convinced them to let her stay. She got her educated and helped her earn her citizenship.

"Elena was totally devoted to Neva. When Neva suffered a stroke, Elena got her administrator's license so she could run the place for her. When Neva passed, she left everything to Elena. And Elena, bless her heart, has always kept to Neva's code."

"She sure does," Steve said. "Without Elena, Clarence and I would be fighting for space under a bridge somewhere."

Olivia nodded. "Me too. I'd been living in my car for most of two weeks when it finally quit running right over there in the parking lot behind the Soda Springs Big Store. And y'all, I was just a hot mess. I only had what I had tossed in my car after I shot my ex-husband and lit out for this end of the country."

All three teen mouths dropped open. "You shot your ex-husband?" Soosie asked.

"Yeah. If ever there was a man who needed a good killing, it was that snake-mean bastard. Unfortunately, I was a little too riled to aim accurately, so he lived.

"Anyway, I was just a sitting there bawling my eyes out when Elena came over. Next thing, she put me up in one of the rooms upstairs, gave me room and board while I got certified as an aide, and then began paying me too. I've been here four years, and frankly I want to stay here until it's time for me to move downstairs and let somebody else wait on me. It's why I agreed to their fool plan," she said as she flipped her hand in the direction of the men.

The front door began to rattle as someone tried the handle. It was followed by the sound of someone pushing on the automatic opener several times. Finally, frustration sounded in the hard raps against the door. It was Chief Braden's voice they heard calling through the door.

"Mr. Hirsch? Are you there?"

David maneuvered around the occupants at the table and over to the door. "What you need, Ben?"

"Before we register them as runaways, is there any chance the three teenagers from Pittison House are in there with you?"

David looked at the three young people. There was acute unease on each of their faces.

"Yup. We're giving them lessons in civil disobedience, and they're helping wipe our asses."

"Could I talk to them?"

After a moment, Myron got up from the loveseat and crossed to the door. "Sir, this is Myron Tatum."

"Myron, you and the other kids understand there are repercussions for leaving Pittison without permission, don't you?"

"Yes, sir. We know."

"I don't suppose you would be willing to come out now and let me take you back."

"Thank you, sir, but I think we need to stay here," Myron said as he looked at Adam and Soosie, who both nodded in agreement.

"I'm not sure I can do anything to help you out after tonight," Chief Braden warned.

"Yes, sir. We understand."

The chief's boots could be heard crossing the porch and stepping down the stairs.

David looked around at each of the kids. "You know that was your get out of jail free card you just gave up."

By eight thirty, the teens had helped Olivia get Clarence, Bert, Tilly, and Katie settled for the night. Returning to the office with the pill tray, Olivia stopped in the main room. She eyed the three kids. "Where y'all going to sleep?"

"Here, I guess," Myron said. "Adam and I can use the recliners, and Soosie's short enough that she can use the loveseat." The other two shrugged their acquiescence with the plan.

"You kids bring any civvies with you? If so, you might wanna change. The thermostat is programmed to turn the heat down at night. It might get a little cool in here in just scrubs."

Taking turns in the bathroom, Soosie and Adam emerged wearing jeans and sweatshirts. Myron changed into his usual khakis and a sweater.

Olivia turned the lamp on the desk to a low setting before heading to the door leading to the staircase. She pointed to a button beside the door jamb. "This rings upstairs. Usually nobody needs anything in the night—at least according to our graveyard staff. However, if anything happens, just ring this, and I'll be down in a jiff. Sleep tight."

Adam and Myron pushed the recliners on either side of the loveseat back. Soosie curled up on the loveseat. In moments, they were all asleep.

Chapter 28

The early morning light filtering through the vertical blinds pulled Adam from sleep. Turning his head, he opened his eyes. Across from him, Myron was still asleep with his arms folded over his chest and his head tilted down in Adam's direction. Soosie was also still curled up with her arm tucked under head like a pillow. She had pulled out her ponytail elastic, and her blonde hair splayed across the dark brown leather.

He heard a door open and the faint squeak of Paul's walker crossing the hall followed by a spill of light from the kitchen.

Carefully lowering the footrest, Adam slipped out of the recliner. In the laundry room, he dug fresh scrubs and his kit out of Myron's duffle before heading to the bathroom.

The quiet thunk of the recliner's footrest lowering near her head penetrated Soosie's sleep, and she awoke with a start. Stretching, she looked over the end of the loveseat. Myron's profile was a silhouette against the early morning light. As she watched, he slowly opened his eyes and stared at the ceiling. He didn't turn his head when she swung to a sitting position and then launched herself in the direction of the hall.

Soosie came into the laundry as Adam was stuffing his jeans, sweatshirt, and kit back into the duffle. He shoved it in her direction before heading to the kitchen. Myron was waiting his turn when she returned.

Having changed as well, Myron was just placing the duffle on the chair by the maintenance cabinet when Olivia stuck her head in the laundry room. "Well, don't you all look bright-eyed and bushy-tailed this morning. Ready to get at it?"

The morning routine went only a little smoother than the previous day. Adam was clearing the table when Olivia and Soosie arrived with their breakfast trays. Bert had pushed herself away from the table and was banging her hands on the arms of her wheelchair.

"Myron, would mind putting Miss Bert in that spot of sunlight peeking through the blinds? She just loves sitting in the morning sun and she can't understand why we aren't taking her to the porch like we usually do."

David and his laptop were once again occupying the small table. "Hey, somebody started a Twitter account on our behalf! The hashtag is '#go granny go,' and there are over a hundred messages giving us a thumbs up for, and I quote, not giving in to the man, end quote."

Emily poured herself another cup of coffee. "Well, the man is supposed to show up Monday, and I'm concerned that if we try to keep him or her locked out, the state will just pull Elena's license and haul us all out without even doing an inspection."

"Olivia, what exactly needs to be done to pass the inspection?" Myron asked.

She took a long pull of her sweet tea, and her brow wrinkled in thought. "Well, first of all, everything must be spit-spot clean, from the building to the residents. All the records must be current and complete. They look for safety issues, like loose grab bars. Stuff like that."

Myron looked at Adam and Soosie. "Okay, we have two days to get the cleaning done. Olivia, if you can show us what we should do on the cleaning, we'll do it."

"I don't know if you can. I'm still gonna need you to help with the residents, and Paul's gonna need help in the kitchen, plus the laundry."

"Well, show us anyway, and we can give it our best shot."

Olivia led them to the empty room down the hall and pointed out everything—from dusting everywhere, including under the beds, to washing walls and floors, scrubbing bathrooms, and making sure all the bedding was fresh and clean.

"You are going to need to talk to Paul about the kitchen. He should remember what it took to pass inspections from when he owned Shorty's Grubstake."

Myron looked at the other two teens and drew a deep breath. "Okay, Soosie, if you can work on the front hall rooms, I'll start in the back room and then move on to the guys' rooms. Adam, since you're helping Paul anyway, maybe you could tackle the kitchen."

"You kids are real determined, aren't you? Well, then I'll tackle the office and make sure all the records are up to snuff. At least nobody can say we didn't try. "

Everyone worked steadily through the morning. By lunch, Soosie had cleaned the empty room and Bert's room. Myron had finished the back room plus Steve and Clarence's room, and was ready to start Paul's room. Adam had cleaned one wall of cabinets in between hunting and fetching items for Paul. Olivia reported she was nearly done bringing all the medical records to current as she and Soosie headed to feed Tilly and Katie.

When Emily and Mary arrived at the dining room table, they reported there were now numerous news vans and reporters outside the center and the curious observers were considerably more numerous than yesterday.

"Probably because it's the weekend and there isn't much else happening. We're up to over five hundred comments on Twitter, and we have about a thousand Likes on our Facebook page," David said.

"And you're not going to believe this, but there is a whole group of people who are parked in the Big Store lot, and it looks like they're having some kind of tailgate party," Emily said.

Myron choked on the bite he had just taken. Steve began to pound his back. He closed his eyes as he recovered his breath.

"Are you okay?" Mary asked.

"Sorry, but that sounds like something my family would do. 'Never pass up an occasion to party' is sorta big in the family code."

Mary got up. "You can take a peek from my window if you want."

Myron followed her to her room and looked out through the blinds. Stepping back, he sighed. "That's them."

"Well?" Paul asked when they resumed their places.

Myron nodded dejectedly. "Yeah. They're probably celebrating my coming out—as a criminal."

It was leaning on eight p.m. when Olivia stepped into the laundry room. All the young people looked exhausted but were gamely still folding the laundry.

"Myron, would you mind getting Clarence into bed, and Soosie, let's make sure Tilly and Katie are comfortable. And then, kids, you are done. No more work today."

As the three trudged out of the laundry room, Olivia flipped off the light. She and Soosie headed to the back room while Myron went to Steve and Clarence's.

* * * * *

Steve looked up from the book he was reading aloud to Clarence. "You kids busted butt today. Elena's pretty particular about our rooms, but damn, man, I think you could safely eat off the floors!"

Fatigue was evident in Myron's smile as he got Clarence transferred and changed for the night. He was almost staggering as he made his way up the hall.

When he turned into the main room, he found Adam already asleep on the loveseat, one foot on the floor, as if he had sat down and simply toppled over. Curled on her side, Soosie was also already asleep in the recliner. Neither of them had changed out of their scrubs. He totally got that. All he wanted to do was just fall into the other recliner, but he made his way back to the laundry room. He pulled his sweater out and tugged it over his scrubs. Then rooting around, he pulled out a fleece jacket he had tossed in and one of Adam's hoodies.

Once more he trekked to the main room. When he got there, he found Mary spreading a lap robe over Adam's shoulders. She straightened and smiled at Myron. "It may be spring, but the nights still get pretty chilly," she said quietly. Stepping to where Myron was standing, she gave him a hug and a kiss on his cheek. "Thank you for being his friend," she whispered. Then she headed back down the front hall.

Myron carefully tucked his fleece jacket around Soosie. He dropped Adam's hoodie on the table, and he finally crawled into the other recliner. He didn't even remember pushing it back.

Chapter 29

Adam awoke with a start and sat up. He was surprised to find himself on the loveseat. He remembered he was only going to sit down for a moment before changing his clothes—and that was all he remembered.

A small quilt had fallen into his lap. He picked it up, puzzled. Glancing to his right, he saw Myron asleep in a sweater he had pulled on over his scrubs. Looking left, Soosie was burrowed under a jacket he recognized as Myron's.

Adam stood up and carefully folded the quilt before laying it on the table. He headed to the laundry room for his stuff and then to the bathroom.

Myron was up and in the laundry room folding Adam's hoodie when he returned from the bathroom.

"I got this out to give you last night, but Mary had already covered you up. FYI, I think she's up." He handed him the quilted lap robe he had picked up from the table.

Adam nodded. He passed Soosie, who was coming through the door still rubbing her eyes and with Myron's jacket slung over her arm.

Mary's door was open. She was standing at the window, peeking between the vertical blinds. "Not much action yet," she said as she carefully let the strip settle into place. "Did you sleep well?"

Adam held out the lap robe. "Yes. Thank you."

Mary took it and opened the doors of the curio cabinet to store it away. "Soosie worked so hard on this room yesterday I'm afraid of messing it up before tomorrow's inspection."

"Yeah, tomorrow…" His voice trailed off.

"Do you have any idea of where you might be placed if they pull you out of Pittison?"

He shook his head.

"How did you end up there anyway?"

"I'm a thrownaway, you know, kid ditched on the streets."

"What a horrible term! What would possess a parent to do that?"

"I guess it's what people do with their 'worst mistakes.'" he said. He couldn't mask the deep pain penetrating his words.

"Why would you think you were someone's worst mistake?" Mary asked, appalled.

"Velma used to tell me that a lot. Said I had totally screwed up both her and Iris's lives."

"Who are they?"

"My mom and grandmother."

"Where was your father?"

Adam looked at Joe's photo. "No clue."

"Do you mind explaining?"

Something in her gentle, probing tone seemed to give Adam permission to lower the defenses he so assiduously maintained against the world. He found the story pouring out of him.

His pain was reflected in her eyes as she listened to him. "I am no longer surprised to hear of women who don't seem to have a single fiber of maternalism in their being. And all those tropes of race, creed, color, religion, sexual orientation etc. have no bearing on it at all. You know Tilly and Katie in the back ward?"

Adam nodded.

"They met at Oregon State University back in the fifties. Both of them had a passion for agriculture, and they developed a passion for each other during their time at college. When they left, they became partners in every sense of the word. They purchased some land together, named it Sweet Frills, and planted the first of their irises. In time, they would earn worldwide recognition for their flower propagation.

"In the sixties, Katie's sister gave birth to a girl with a severe cognitive disability. When the two women went to see the new mother, she dumped the child in Katie's arms and told her, 'You can have her if you want; otherwise, she's going to an institution.'

"They were amazing mothers to the girl, giving her as full a life as she could have under the circumstances. She was always beautifully dressed and spotless. They took her everywhere without embarrassment or apology. They were so proud of her.

"The law office I worked for handled their business, and they always brought her when they came for an appointment. They just doted on a child who had no ability to give anything back."

"Where is she now?"

"She died shortly after her fourteenth birthday. Children who have severe cognitive issues usually have physical ones as well. Even though they knew it was always a probability, they were still utterly devastated."

"I think the only thing that devastated Iris was I didn't die," Adam said bitterly.

"This is going to sound very selfish, and it probably is, but I am very glad Iris and Velma threw you away. If they hadn't, then I would never have had the opportunity to know you."

Adam looked at Joe's portrait again. The looping question he had had since he first saw the picture played across his face.

Mary followed his gaze. "I don't know if Joe was a sperm donor or not, Adam. There was much of his life I was never privy to. It doesn't matter to me if we share any genes or not. All I care about now is you ended up in my life." She paused. "And I would very much like to keep you in it, if that works for you."

They locked eyes, and then he bobbed his head as a self-conscious smile formed.

Soosie appeared in the doorway. "There you are. Paul is throwing a fit because his right-hand man is missing from the kitchen."

Mary laughed. "Tell him he better have the coffee on. Emily and I are headed his way, and we can show him what real fits look like."

Chapter 30

B y lunch time, Myron and Soosie had finished with the private rooms, and Myron had polished the floors in the back hall and back room after Steve provided instruction on how to operate the floor polisher. Adam finished cleaning the kitchen so well even Paul couldn't find fault.

Following a brief conference, it was decided Myron would polish the front hall while Adam cleaned the laundry room and Soosie worked on the laundry. Later, they would all three tackle the main room and then finish all the laundry they could.

Soosie had several stacks of clothes on the folding table when Adam announced he wanted to give the floor of the laundry room a good scrubbing.

"Since we're going to be using it later today, it's just gonna get messed up again," Soosie said.

"I know, but it'll be easier to just give it a quick mop in the morning if it's already pretty clean," he answered. "We're gonna have to be moving fast to make sure everything is done if the inspector is going to be here at nine a.m."

"Yeah, I guess so. Just let me stuff what's in the washer into the dryer, then I'll take these to Emily while you mop."

Myron had apparently finished the front hall since he was polishing the floor around the front door and office when Soosie went by.

"Knock, knock," Soosie said at Emily's open door.

Emily turned away from the window. "Come on in. I'm just checking out what's happening on the streets. Not much in the way of media today, and the gawkers are fewer, although it looks like a lot of Myron's family is back. You know, they may be Soda Springs' black sheep, but overall they are one good-looking family. There is a young couple over there that is just gorgeous, and their baby is adorable. Come see."

Soosie set Emily's laundry on the bed then went over to peek though the vertical blinds. When she saw the back of the young woman handing a toddler to the tall blond man next to her, her gut told her it was the same person who had showed up at the Pitt. She couldn't be absolutely sure until the man nestled the small child's bottom in the crook of his elbow and leaned over to kiss the woman. Finally, the woman turned around. Yup. It was Barbie with her own Ken doll.

A breeze picked up for a moment, catching the sun hat the small child was wearing. It lifted the hat off and sent it into the crowd of people in the parking lot. Another child grabbed it and ran it back to the couple, handing it off to the young woman. As the man turned so she could put the hat back on the little one, Soosie's eyes widened. The child appeared to have microcephaly, just like Sammy.

She peered closer. The child actually looked like Sammy! Her brain began to scream in protest as she spun around and sprinted to the main room.

Myron was looping the cord over the handle of the polisher when she grabbed his arm and pulled him around to look at her.

"Does Barbie have Sammy?"

Myron looked baffled. "Who's Barbie?"

"Your cousin or whoever that person was who came to see you at the Pitt."

"Vivienne?"

"Okay, Vivienne. She's out there with some guy, and he's holding a baby that looks like Sammy."

"If Vivienne and Trevor have a little one with them, yes, it probably is Sammy."

"How the hell did they get their hands on him? What are they going to do with him?" Soosie demanded.

"His dad requested he be placed with them."

"Tyler? But you said Tyler's in jail."

"He is, but your sister put his name on the birth certificate, so after she signed off, the state had to get him to sign off as well. He refused unless Sammy was placed with one of the family."

"I can't believe the state would even consider a Tatum—"

There was a crash behind her as Adam slammed his cleaning caddy down on the table. "Geez, girl, are you Tatum trashing again? I don't see where you Fretwells get off thinking you're so much better. If you were, then this discussion wouldn't even be happening. But it is, because your sister went to jail and you ended up being diverted out of detention. So what I want to know is how you think you are so superior to Myron's family?"

Soosie opened her mouth but stopped, discomfited.

Myron reached out and touched her chin, trying to get her to look at him. He hastily pulled his hand back when she snapped her teeth at him. "Soosie, Vivenne has a master's degree in special education. She works for the Education Service District overseeing all the special ed programs in the Clackamas County schools. Trevor is an attorney who specializes in real estate and business law. They make good money—honest money. Plus, as a member of the Tatum family, Sammy is guaranteed to be surrounded by people who will always have his back."

Soosie shot him a disbelieving look.

"Yeah, that's the way we roll in Tatumland. And you will be able to see Sammy if you want. Your sister is blocked from ever having contact with him, but Viv and Trevor would welcome you to be part of Sammy's life—if you learn to behave yourself."

She looked away when tears sprang to her eyes. "I didn't think I would ever see Sammy again because of...of everything." Suddenly she turned and grabbed the front of Myron's scrub top, pulling him over until she could kiss him.

Startled, they both reared back. Then, staring into each other's eyes, they again leaned in until their faces were only inches apart, their breathing intensifying with each passing moment. Myron slowly lowered his head until he could capture her lips again. She let go of his shirt and slid her arms up and around his neck while he pulled her in tight against him.

Adam stared wide-eyed. "Okay. I did not see that coming."

Paul stumped around the corner and stopped. "What is going on? May I remind you people that we are still in the middle of a war."

Emily and Mary stood side by side in the front hall watching as well. They spoke as one. "Paul, shut up."

Finally, Myron and Soosie broke apart. Stepping back, they kept their eyes downcast, avoiding looking directly at each other. Soosie's hands still rested on Myron's arms, and his hands encircled her waist. Abruptly, she pulled away and bolted in the direction of the back hall.

Emily and Mary exchanged knowing looks. "I'll go," Emily said.

Myron looked dazed, and his breathing was ragged. Adam approached him, waving his hand in front of Myron's face.

"Hey, are you okay? Can I get you anything, like a cold shower or something?"

Myron's eyes slowly cleared, and his breathing became even. He finally focused on Adam's face. "Did that just happen? Did I just kiss Soosie Fretwell?"

"Ah, yeah."

Myron looked down at his hands and shook his head. "Why did I do that?"

"Maybe because you're male and she's female. How the hell do I know why you kissed her? But you seemed to be having a good time doing it."

"I totally was," Myron whispered as he touched his mouth.

When Emily arrived at the laundry room, Soosie had her elbows on the folding table and her face buried in her hands. Emily lightly touched her shoulder.

Soosie lowered her arms to the table, keeping her eyes focused on the opposite wall. "I cannot believe I just kissed Myron."

"Why not?" Emily asked. "He's the absolute walking cliché of every romance novel every written: tall, dark, and definitely handsome."

"He's a Tatum, and Tatums are my sworn enemy."

Emily chuckled. "My dear, that is so melodramatic. I would definitely have red-lined those words if I had found them in an assignment." She paused as she studied the young woman's expression of woe. "Would you mind telling me what Myron has done to warrant your purported aversion?"

"It's not Myron exactly. It's another Tatum, and my sister, and it's—"

"Complicated, I know." Emily leaned on the folding table and rested her chin in her hand as she kept her eyes on Soosie, quietly waiting.

Haltingly at first, the story of the disasters that had befallen the Fretwell family eventually came out in torrents, up to and including the revelations that had just been made. Finally, the words stopped.

"I do believe your thinking is all wrong, Soosie, although I do see how you would have come to the conclusions you did early on. I think the fact a Tatum fathered Sammy may be the best thing that could have happened."

Soosie whipped her head in Emily's direction, her expression a protest.

"Let's look at it. From what Myron has said to you and what you have seen with your own eyes, apparently the Tatums are a group who take their familial duties very seriously. Your sister was the one who couldn't give up her parental rights fast enough if it meant saving her own butt. And yet Tyler was the one whose demands provided protection for the child he apparently didn't even know he had. Because of him, Sammy is not currently at the mercy of the foster system. He is instead with two very responsible people who have the knowledge and means to help him reach his highest potential. And I suspect Myron had a hand in it somewhere as well. Why else would his cousin show up to talk with him?"

Emily let her words sink into Soosie before she continued softly.

"You're angry, Soosie. Life took a dogleg when your dad had his accident. And instead of your mother stepping up and being the adult for you and your sister, she reverted to being the one who expected to be cared for by two girls who weren't ready or equipped for such responsibility.

"Regardless of her taste for bad boys, what Stevie was looking for was someone to take care of her as well. I agree there were all kinds of judgment errors resulting in Sammy, but I think being saddled with a child she hadn't planned or wanted only fueled her anger, especially when Tyler seemingly vanished and left her alone with even more responsibility.

"And you were caught in the middle of everything, trying desperately to hold it all together with no support from anyone. No wonder you blew up like you did. But I think if you think about it, the people you're really angry with are your mom and sister for failing to make any effort and your dad for leaving you in such a mess."

Soosie shot Emily a look falling somewhere between denial and guilt.

Emily smiled. "It's okay. Anger is a normal part of the grieving process, but a part most people don't want to admit to. Yet it must be owned and worked through, or the process will never be complete. So be angry; your dad wouldn't mind. He may even have had a little hostility himself when he found himself on the other side."

The moments stretched as Soosie examined Emily's words. Finally she asked in a small voice, "Do I still hate Myron?"

Emily gave her a hug. "I don't know. The answer is in you, sweetie. But I would like to know what it is when you figure it out."

Chapter 31

The rest of the day wore on awkwardly as Soosie and Myron went out of their way to pretend the other wasn't in the room. Adam wasn't sure if he should laugh or be irritated with the pair of them. But despite the side-stepping and other avoidance strategies, they still managed to get the main room cleaned.

Adam had just dragged the last garbage bag to the back door when Paul hollered for him. It was beginning to be a fairly substantial pile they would have to haul to the dumpster early in the morning. David had prohibited them from unjamming any of the doors since various ones had been rattled throughout the weekend.

As Adam headed to the kitchen, he took a quick peek into the laundry room. Myron and Soosie had their backs to each other. Whatever hung in the air between them was thick enough to cut. Shaking his head, Adam backtracked to the kitchen.

After finishing the evening duties, the three teens had just returned to the laundry room when Olivia appeared in the doorway with a stack of towels and washcloths in her arms.

"I know y'all have been making do with spit baths in the bathroom since you got here, but I thought maybe a real, honest-to-gosh shower would feel good tonight."

Welcome moans met her suggestion.

"Thought so. Who wants to be first?"

"Myron, you're pretty much done. Why don't you go first," Adam said.

Myron pulled the blue duffel off the chair and dug out fresh clothes and his kit before following Olivia out of the room.

Soosie finished loading the dryer before digging out her plastic bag. She pulled the elastic out of her ponytail and ran her hand through her hair to fluff it.

Myron returned carrying his scrubs, wet towel, and kit. "Next."

Soosie looked at Adam. He motioned at her stuff. "Go for it."

Adam and Myron finished folding a pile of sheets they had pulled from the dryer. Myron offered to put them away so Adam could be ready for his shower.

Adam grabbed his stuff. "I'll wait up front," he said.

Myron returned to the laundry room. He put his wet towels in the washing machine and left the door open to load everyone else's. He dragged out the pile of dirty scrubs they had been kicking under the chair and loaded the small machine as well.

Soosie came in the room with her head wrapped in a towel. She tossed her bag, wet towel, and dirty scrubs on the folding table. Silently, Myron picked them up and placed them in the machines.

Bending over, she vigorously damp-dried her hair. Straightening up, she flipped it back from her face. Soosie balled the towel up and pitched it across the table into the open machine before digging in her bag and pulling out her comb. She began trying to get the comb through her wet hair. It caught in the snarls and, as Myron watched, she began to rip viciously at the tangles.

"Stop. Stop," he said as he came around the table and caught her hand, forcing her to relinquish the comb. "You're just making it worse. Let me do it."

Soosie skewered him with her eyes. "Riiiight. You know about untangling hair."

He pulled the chair out and lightly pushed on her shoulders from behind, forcing her to sit. "Actually, I do. Mom had no patience, and Lucy was a wigglebutt, so I usually combed her hair out…" His voice became so soft she almost couldn't hear him. "Until there was none to comb."

As he carefully lifted sections and teased each snarl down the length until the hair fell smooth, Soosie closed her eyes and just concentrated on the feel of his hands in her hair and on her back when they occasionally brushed it.

Finally he was done. She opened her eyes and saw he was holding her comb in front of her face. She reached out to take it.

"You really loved your sister, didn't you?" she asked, as she turned in the chair to look up at him.

"Yes." That single word came from someplace so deep in him Soosie felt rather than heard it.

Soosie thought about her sister. Did she love Stevie? She disliked her selfishness and immaturity. She hated her for what she had done to Sammy. She resented her for always being able to manipulate their mother into letting her have or do whatever she wanted. She realized maybe she didn't love her sister, at least not the way she supposed people should. Was that her failing or Stevie's?

When Adam came in, Myron held out his hand for the towels. "Scrubs are in the other machine." He added them to the load and started the washer while Adam finished loading and starting the other washer. Soosie put the chair back.

Without speaking, the three left the laundry room and headed up front. Myron stopped to turn the table lamp to low. Adam settled into the recliner while Soosie curled up on the loveseat. Myron pushed back in the other recliner.

Unlike the previous nights when they had fallen asleep almost before they had fully stretched out, slumber proved more elusive tonight as each of them wondered where they would be when tomorrow ended. Yet, despite the dread circling their thoughts, the physical activity of the day eventually swept them into sleep.

Soosie awoke with a start. In the low light of the lamp, she could see Adam asleep when she looked over the end of the loveseat. She craned her neck back to see Myron. It gave her a weird perspective of his sleeping form.

Even though she knew it was irrational, she had been afraid to think about the kiss she had shared with him while the two young men were awake; like they would be able to see into her brain or something. Now she closed her eyes and relived it.

She had had her share of kisses: awkward, sloppy, aggressive, perfunctory. Myron's was different. It felt like the kind of kiss a man, not a boy, would give. It made her feel both wanted and yet safe. How bizarre; the only times she actually felt safe were when she was around Myron. That was just wrong on so many levels, and yet there it was.

She opened her eyes and watched the reflected headlights of a passing car roll across the room's ceiling. When they disappeared, she felt chilled. Tomorrow was the big unknown and she was scared. How she hated to admit it even to herself. She curled tighter into herself, as though if she made herself small enough, tomorrow would pass over her without noticing her existence.

Tears gathered behind her eyelids. All she wanted was to feel like everything would be okay; that she would come out on the other side safe and whole. She needed…she needed arms.

She got up and moved to the space between the end of the loveseat and the recliner Myron was sleeping in. She watched him for a moment. Then, sitting on the arm, she swung her legs around and slid her body down beside his.

When he roused, she put her fingers over his mouth. "Shhh," she whispered. Slipping her hand down to rest on his chest, she wriggled until she could nestle her head on his shoulder.

He answered by placing one hand over hers and wrapping his other arm around her.

She sighed deeply and slept.

Chapter 32

Early morning sunlight was edging around the vertical blinds. Myron's mind skated on the shimmery surface between sleep and waking. Feeling someone under his arm, he thought it was Lucy, once again cuddled against his body because she had gotten scared in the night. But as he inched closer to wakefulness, he realized it was Soosie who lay against him.

Somewhere in their sleep, they had turned on their sides so her bottom was pushed into his pelvis. He jolted to full consciousness when a fire, having nothing to do with brotherly feelings, exploded through him.

Bracing his hand on the opposite chair arm, he was able to lever himself carefully out of the chair without significantly disturbing his companion. As he watched Soosie sleep, he was totally aware of his desire to kiss her and not stop.

Blowing out a shaky breath, he headed to the bathroom to splash cold water on his face. It wasn't a smart move letting those feelings take root in either his mind or his body. Today, it all would end, and they were not likely to be in proximity of each other by tomorrow.

Coming out of the bathroom, he headed down to the laundry room and flipped on the lights. He transferred the wet towels and scrubs to their respective dryers. Then, taking the broom, he swept the floor.

David had decreed the doors could not be unbarred until 6, and the clock said 5:17, so he couldn't take the garbage to the dumpster. He heard a noise next door and saw the kitchen light go on. He wandered into the kitchen and saw Paul wearing a sleeveless sundress in lollipop-colored stripes with a white scalloped collar filling the coffee pot with water. He glanced at Myron as he headed to the coffeemaker. "You're up early."

Myron gestured to his attire. "I guess that means the war is over."

"For the time being. We'll see after the inspection. And speaking of that, sorry about interrupting your," he hooked his fingers in the air, 'moment.'"

Myron looked at him blankly.

"Okay, that must have been some kiss if you didn't even hear an old man kvetching at you."

Myron blushed as he looked away. "It was pretty amazing."

"It's because she's a spitfire. You kiss one of them and it takes kissing to a whole new level because you never know if they're going to kiss back or scratch your eyeballs out."

"Voice of experience?"

"Damn right. My Gayle was hell on wheels. Our fights were the stuff of legends. So was our making up. We scrapped our way through forty-seven years before I lost her to ovarian cancer."

Paul held out the skirt of his dress. "She made this. She was an absolute whiz with the sewing machine. She'd see something she liked, and two days later she'd be wearing it. She never saw a fabric store she didn't want to dive into. We had mountains of sewing stuff everywhere. Couldn't hardly sit in a chair without finding a pin or needle stuck in your ass."

The coffee finished brewing, and Paul poured a cup. He held it out to Myron, who shook his head. "Thanks. No."

Paul took a sip. "In one of those strange twists life slings at you, one of the last things she asked before cancer took over our lives was to check the outlet she kept her sewing machine plugged into. She told me it smelled hot. Of course, like any good husband, I put it off. Then it got shoved out of my mind entirely.

"Five months after I buried Gayle, I ended up standing outside our home in my skivvies watching our entire life together go up in flames from a short in the wiring. All I had left was what was in the detached garage. Gayle kept her old clothes stashed in totes there. I dug out the most butch thing I could find, which ended being a pair of pedal pushers and a top. The odd thing was, the minute I did, it was like she was with me again. I could smell her, feel her, hear her. I decided that if, by gum, all I had left were memories, then I would wear them literally every day the rest of my life. Battle situations excepted."

"I get that. After my sister died and all the medical equipment that had been in her room was taken away, I went in and made everything just the way she liked it. Sometimes I would go in and pretend she and I were playing. I would even pretend to have the same arguments we did before…" Myron looked embarrassed. "It sounds really dumb but she didn't feel so…so dead then."

"Nobody is ever completely dead until there is no one left to remember them. None of us here at the center have much of anyone to even remember we're alive now, let alone give us a thought after we're gone. You're all young with lots of years still to be lived, so I guess you three are stuck with being our only legacy."

Myron grinned. "I'm okay with that, and I'm pretty sure I'm not ever going to forget you."

* * * * *

Returning to the laundry room just as the dryer with the scrubs inside clicked off, Myron pulled them out and began to sort and fold them in piles of blue, green, and pastels.

Adam came through the door. "Dude, Soosie is in your recliner. Did you two sleep together last night?"

"She crawled in sometime after I was asleep. I didn't really notice until this morning when I woke up."

"You're telling me she squeezed into a small space with you and you didn't notice?"

"I guess my brain was flashing back to Lucy. She would always come get in my bed when she got scared. After she got so sick, I would sleep on the floor by her bed so if she got scared, I could just get in her bed with her."

"And that explains Soosie how?"

"I'm thinking maybe she was upset, you know, because of today."

"Uh-huh." Adam sounded dubious.

"Listen, absolutely nothing happened. I slept, she slept. I got up. She was still sleeping."

Looking for an excuse to change the subject, Myron looked at the clock. It was now just a few minutes before six a.m.

David stopped next to the door. "Okay, you can open the back doors."

"Come on, let's get the garbage in the dumpster before we change," Myron said.

When they returned, they found Soosie in the laundry room along with Olivia. Soosie was pale, but her tough-girl face was in place. Olivia looked on the verge of tears.

"I'm real sorry, kids, but Chief Braden is here, and he wants you to gather up your stuff and report to him right this minute," Olivia said.

Chapter 33

The three teens exchanged resigned looks. Myron picked up the duffle from the folding table where Soosie had put it while getting her brush out. He gently took the brush from her hand, stuffed it in her bag, and zipped the duffle.

Swinging it off the table, he took the lead out the door with Adam and Soosie trailing. From the hall they could see Chief Braden waiting by the reception desk. His thumbs were hooked in his utility belt, and his face was stern as he watched them.

When they reached the desk, he said nothing. He just crossed to the front door, now stripped of its protest sign, and opened it.

"Why, thank you, Chief," Emily and Mary said as they came in.

"You're out early for your walk today, ladies," he said.

"Yes. We haven't been for several days, so we wanted to get it in before inspectors, media, the Wicked Witch of the West, and whoever else show up."

Stepping into the room, Emily and Mary suddenly noticed the kids standing silently by. They extrapolated what was occurring.

Emily looked at the chief. "I just want you to know I am officially protesting the arrest of these young people."

"I'm not arresting them. I am returning them to Pittison House. It will be up to the house counselors what happens."

"If you're not arresting them, then are they free to walk out of here?" Emily demanded.

"They are minors who are under the supervision and protection of the state, so they aren't free to walk anywhere for the time being," he answered with a sigh.

While Emily was arguing with the chief, Mary walked over to the kids. She gave each of them a hug, ending with Adam. For the first time, he returned the hug. He whispered in her ear, "I'm sorry."

She placed her hands on either side of his face and looked into his eyes. "I have never been prouder of anyone in my whole life," she said softly.

While Emily continued to natter at him, the chief pulled the door open wider and motioned the kids toward it. "Let's go."

David was parked in his favorite location and enjoying his cigar when the kids crossed the porch and stepped down to the sidewalk. He called to the chief. "You know this is just wrong, Ben," he said. "These kids busted ass taking care of us and doing everything humanly possible to make sure we're gonna keep our home."

Chief Braden sighed again. "It doesn't matter what I think, Mr. Hirsch. I don't make the rules. I just enforce them."

Following the kids down, he opened the back door of his patrol car. "Myron and Adam, you in the back. Soosie, you sit up front with me."

As the car pulled away, the three took one last look at the center. David, Paul, Emily, and Mary all lined the porch grimly watching their departure.

In a few minutes, the car pulled up in front of the Pitt. Chief Braden came around and opened both doors. Adam crawled out then reached back for the duffle so Myron could get out. Soosie climbed out.

Stepping back, Chief Braden swung his hand in the direction of the front door.

"Thank you, sir," Myron said and, squaring his shoulders, led the way. Just as he reached for the door handle, the door flew open. Dustin stood there.

"Welcome back. Just so you know where you stand, your asses are grass, and I am the official lawnmower. To the office. Now." He waved to the chief, who had maintained a position on the sidewalk. Closing the door, he followed the teens to the office.

Lined up on the couch, the faces on all three were a mixture of fear and defiance. Dustin picked up three files from the desk before sitting in one of the office chairs and swinging around to face them.

He gave them a long serious look. "Anyone got anything they want to say to me?"

Myron stood up, edging sideways until he was partially shielding both Soosie and Adam. "Everything that happened was because of me," he said. "I was the one who provided information about what was being planned. I was the one who decided to get involved."

"So you're telling me Adam and Soosie are innocent. That you what? Coerced? Threatened? Blackmailed them into going with you?"

Adam stood up as well. "No, Myron didn't do any of those things. I volunteered because I knew how to bypass the alarm so I could get us out of here without getting caught."

Dustin's eyes widened. "You? I assumed it was—never mind. May I ask how long you've known how to override the security system?"

Adam gave a small smile. "Since about my third month here, when one of the other kids threw something and knocked the cover off so I could see its innards."

"And how often have you gone AWOL without us knowing?" Adam just looked over Dustin's head and gave a small, noncommittal shrug of a shoulder. "Okay, obviously, until this last time, you always came back, so it isn't really relevant right now."

Although it was hard to see her behind the two young men, Dustin leaned forward and asked. "Soosie? You have anything to say?"

She elbowed her way into a standing position. "They weren't going to take me, but I made them."

"Did any of you talk to Chief Braden last Friday?"

"Yes," Myron answered.

"So you know that you had an opportunity to return without facing any consequences, and you voluntarily declined the offer."

All three nodded while staring into the air above Dustin's head.

Dustin studied them for a long moment. "So all three of you are admitting you willfully and volitionally chose to leave Pittison without permission and subsequently barricade yourself in the Soda Springs Care Center, where you have remained for the last three-plus days. You also are stating that when you were offered a chance to be returned, courtesy of Chief Braden on Friday, you refused. Am I correct?"

They nodded in unison again.

"Okay, I am going to require you three stay in your rooms with the exception of bathroom breaks and meals. Once I have determined the full extent of your violation of house rules, I will arrange a formal hearing on the matter and notify you."

He tossed their files back on his desk and got up. He led the way out of the office. He positioned himself between the stairs and the front door before motioning them to proceed.

At the upper landing, Myron squatted down and opened the duffle. He pulled Soosie's bag out and handed it to her.

It was evident in the look she gave him she wanted to say something, but with Dustin observing, she just took it and headed for the stairs leading to the third floor.

Myron's eyes followed her until she disappeared from view, then he turned and followed Adam into their room.

He dropped the duffle on the floor and sat on his bed. "I'm sorry, man."

"For what?"

"Getting everybody busted."

Adam looked at the ceiling. "Strange, isn't it. We didn't mug anyone, steal a car, or hold up the 7-Eleven. We were actually trying to do something to help other people, and we are just as busted as if we had done the bad things."

"Probably not quite. I'm guessing because we weren't doing bad shit, we'll still age out of the system when we're supposed to, just from a different place than here."

Adam nodded as he chewed the thought over. "You know what's even stranger?"

Myron looked at him questioningly.

"We're probably not even going to know what happens at the center—if all this even did any good."

Chapter 34

When the lunch buzzer rang, the three teens made their way quietly to the dining room and took their usual seats, earning dirty looks from two new residents who thought they had claim on those chairs.

Dustin came out of the office. Oddly, he seemed a little rattled as he made his announcement. "Okay, you are making a preliminary appearance today. After lunch, I want you to clean up and dress appropriately. Chief Braden will be transporting you, so be downstairs no later than 2:15."

Trepidation flowed in the glances the three exchanged.

At 2:10, Myron and Adam came downstairs. Myron was dressed in his usual khakis and an olive-green polo shirt. Adam was wearing his least scruffy jeans and a navy-blue-and-gray-striped polo shirt courtesy of Myron. Both were cleanly shaved, and their thick hair was tamed.

Soosie descended a minute later. She was wearing blue jeans, but she had replaced her usual tee-shirt with a blue-and-pink-paisley top made of material that floated over her arms and her body. She had French-braided her hair and added makeup emphasizing her blue eyes and soft mouth. Instead of the street-tough girl they were used to, this was one who might inspire some mushy poetry from a locker-room Lothario. Even Dustin looked startled by the transformation.

She threw a nervous look to Myron, who stepped back to the bottom step and held his hand out. Soosie clutched at it.

When she reached the main floor, he was the one who slowly extracted his fingers from her grip while she glanced up at him through her eyelashes.

Observing the ploy, Adam mentally shouted out a warning. "Don't do it, man! Don't look in her eyes. You're dead meat if you do!"

The potentially lethal flirt was interrupted by a knock at the door. Dustin opened it for the police chief.

"You kids ready?" the chief asked.

The two young men stood back, allowing Soosie to go first before following. Once again Adam and Myron crawled in the back seat while Soosie sat in front.

Getting behind the wheel, the chief leaned forward to check his side mirror then smoothly pulled away from the curb. It was silent as death as each of the three sat stone still. Finally, the car pulled around the back of a building. The chief got out and opened first the back door and then the front door of the car. The teens got out slowly and huddled together.

He nodded toward the steel door. "Since each of you has been here before, I think you know the way to the reception desk. I'll meet you there after I park the car."

Hesitating outside the doors, the three looked at each other with confusion. Finally, Adam pulled on the handle and the door opened. They could see the reception desk at the other end of the hall.

They advanced slowly, glancing at the doors lining the hall

until they reached the desk. The chief was just entering the building. He motioned them forward.

Myron stepped around the corner first, then reached back, pulling Soosie and Adam up beside him as whoops and shouts greeted them.

Elena rushed to them, enveloping each of them in a hug. "We passed the inspection! Everyone is to stay here. You did such good work the inspector said he would have no fears putting his own mother here."

The front door opened again, and Dustin stepped through. The three kids stared at him. "Cake. I heard there would be cake," he said to them.

They automatically closed ranks and looked at each other, silently wondering what was going on. Was this just a way stop?

David rolled up with an unlit cigar in his mouth. "He tell you yet?" motioning toward Dustin.

They shook their heads.

David pulled a folded piece of paper from beside him, using it to motion Dustin over. "You got something you want to say to these three?"

"Yeah. So, after consideration, we decided you actually did not meet the criteria for being runaways since we knew where you were the entire time you were absent from the Pitt, a fact verified during your conversation with the chief. That means you were technically only guilty of leaving without permission, and you returned willingly. Sorta. So, in light of those circumstances, we are scrubbing everything from your records. You are in the same position as you were before you left last Friday. Fair enough?"

During his speech, Dustin wasn't looking at the teens. He was looking at David, who grinned around the cigar in his mouth and held out the paper. Dustin snatched it. After flipping it open and scanning it, he refolded it before carefully tearing it into small pieces.

David jerked his thumb over his shoulder. "Lots of good food on the table. Dive in."

Dustin tossed a resigned look at the kids before circling around David's wheelchair where Elena was handing out plates.

The three looked back at David. "Just figured all of us needed to sleep in our own beds tonight without worrying about the morrow, so I borrowed a page from Adah's playbook. I wrote a letter purportedly to the editor of the *Sentinel*. It didn't exactly flatter the Pittison House leadership. I emailed it to Dustin with the promise it would be delivered if you three were punished for helping a bunch of old people who couldn't help themselves.

"Now I am going to go enjoy a stress-free cigar. Save some chow for me." He turned his chair toward the front door, and the chief hit the button to open it. David raised a hand as he sailed out onto the porch.

Although it had, in fact, only been a few hours since they left, the teens and the residents were reacting as if it had been days. Unaware that both Dustin and the chief were closely observing their interactions, the teens hugged, shook hands, and kissed their way around the room. Finally, they settled on the loveseat with their plates loaded with food and began to pack it away.

While they were eating, Elena motioned Dustin to her office. When they emerged, he was carrying three plastic bags. Adam was the only one still sitting on the loveseat. Dustin made his way over to him. "Where's Myron and Soosie?" Adam tried to hedge, but Dustin wasn't having any of it. "Look, I was sorta strong-armed into the whole let you three get away with breaking the rules thing, but that can still change."

Sighing, Adam got up and led the way to the back hall. He stopped outside the laundry, loudly clearing his throat before flicking on the lights. Although Soosie and Myron had stepped away from each other, it was evident from their flushed faces what they had been up to.

Dustin goggled at them. "Hormones? When the hell did hormones instead of violence break out between you two?" He flung the three bags on the folding table. "Mrs. Fuentes has requested you three be allowed to continue to work here. Our agreement is you will work here as long as you are living at Pittison. Once you age out, any continued opportunity for employment will be between you and Mrs. Fuentes.

"Now, go back and enjoy your party. When we get back to the Pitt, I'm obviously going to have to wire alarms on some people's doors."

"That won't be necessary, sir," Myron said. "I promise the only person I'm going to sleep with while I am at the Pitt is Adam."

Dustin feigned his eyeballs coming out of his head on stalks. "Is there something you two want to tell me?"

"Thanks, dude. Screw my reputation before I even see if I like kissing girls," Adam said.

Myron looked at Soosie with a huge smile on his face. "Oh, you're definitely going to like it."

Dustin turned away, flapping his hand in their direction. "Do me a favor, you three. Just finish growing up and go away!"

"That is our plan, sir."

ADAM RIDDICK

PH Case No. 2013-03-26

S eptember 18, and today I officially age out. In just a little while, Jarett is going to give me and my garbage bag of stuff a ride to the care center. Since I don't have any place else, Elena has offered to let me stay a few days until I can scrape together some kind of living situation.

Right now I'm sitting on the bed I've slept in for the past three years. I've already stripped it and put everything in the hampers. The bed across from me has been empty since Myron aged out in July. Although I see him five days a week when we work together, the room has felt emptier than it ever did at any time before we shared it.

Elena helped Myron get his certification as a nurse's aide, so he actually isn't doing the cleaning/laundry stuff anymore. Still, he's around, and if I wait until he's done helping feed Tilly and Katie, we have lunch together.

I guess Elena is letting him stay in another little room upstairs where Olivia and Lidiya live. He's been saving up his money and is going to start at Clackamas Community College at the end of the month. He wants to be a nurse and eventually work in pediatrics.

It wasn't so bad the first few weeks after he left because Soosie was still here. We'd hang out in the common room just to give each other some company. But then in August, she got her kicked-out notice and was gone too.

I've hardly seen her since she left. Myron's cousin Vivienne and her husband hired Soosie to care for Sammy during their working hours, so she is no longer working at the care center. Their house had a nanny suite, so Soosie is actually living with them. Once in a while, she comes in at the end of the shift to pick up Myron. Yeah, they're still going hot and heavy. He says she is planning on starting at CCC at the same time he is. She is going to be studying early childhood education, maybe eventually going into special education like Vivienne.

And my great ambition is I would love to learn to cook like Paul. How I'm going to be able to make that happen without having to leave the care center, I don't know. The only people I have are Myron, Mary, and the rest of the people at the center. If I take off to try to find a burger-flipping job, then I'm back to where I started: no place to live and nobody to care whether I am alive.

Okay, it's time. Jarett just handed me the manila envelope with all the papers Velma had stuffed in my backpack, plus my high school diploma.

Deep breath, dude. You're officially a free man.

Jarett gave me a ride to the care center. After pulling the garbage bag out of the car trunk, he told me to check in once in a while and let them know how I was doing. Then I was standing at the foot of the stairs as another part of my past drove away.

I climbed the stairs trying to wrap my brain around the fact I would not be heading back to the Pitt. I was just reaching to push the button when a car horn honked. It was Myron. He stepped out of the car and hollered for me to put my stuff in the laundry room and come try out my new freedom.

Instead of cruising around, he drove straight to a house in one of the nicest areas of Soda Springs. I could see Soosie watching as we parked. As soon as the brake was set, she was there throwing herself in my arms. That was awkward on so many levels, but she just giggled and grabbed my hand, pulling me along.

As we approached the house, a man came out. There was definitely a resemblance between him and Myron, except he was much beefier, and his shock of hair was about equal parts brown and gray.

He introduced himself as Myron's uncle Ralph. "So your Myron's brother from another mother," he said. "Welcome to the family."

Okay, that knocked me on my ass. I looked at Myron. He was wearing his wary face, the one expecting rejection. Right, I was going to reject the only person who had ever given a shit about me in the whole of my life. I said the only thing that came to my mind: "Thank you." Myron pulled me into a hug.

Ralph gave us a moment before announcing, "Well, are we going to party or what?"

"Party?" I asked.

"Dude, you aged out today, so that means it's your birthday. Hell yeah, we're going to party," Myron said as he pushed me toward the backyard.

The whole time it was like I was having an out-of-body experience. People, food, cake, presents—it felt like it was happening to someone else, not the "mistake" who had never had a party in his life.

Finally, Myron and Soosie helped load everything into his car, including me. After some kissing that made me wonder just how long those two could hold their breath, Myron drove us back to the center.

We emptied the trunk and filled our arms. Myron led the way to the upper floor of the house. There, he pushed open the door to the space he was occupying. I almost dropped everything when I walked in. I was expecting something about the size of our room at the Pitt, but this place was *huge*.

Myron explained that, although she was still working at the center, Lidiya had moved in with her daughter and son-in-law to help with the baby. When Elena learned I had no place to go, she decided we should share the space.

Between Elena and what Myron had picked up from his parents' house, the room had everything. Just when I thought I couldn't take in any more, Olivia hollered up the stairs at us.

"Must be time for dinner," Myron said.

I told him I wasn't really hungry yet. He announced I didn't have a choice and to get my butt down the stairs pronto.

Coming out the door at the bottom of the stairs, I found I was the guest of honor at another birthday party. The old people had decorated the dining area with streamers and balloons. They had a birthday cake and ice cream, and they proudly presented me with my own laptop computer. Mary gave me a card with birthday wishes to a grandson. Yeah, I embarrassed myself by tearing up. She slipped me a tissue while giving me a hug. Everybody else pretended not to notice.

Too wound up to fall asleep, I lay in our room listening to Myron's breathing as he slept. It was familiar and comforting. I could see the glow of the smartphone Ralph had handed me at the end of the party. "It's programmed with family phone numbers," he said as he put it in my hand. "You need anything, you push one of those numbers. Us Tatums are always here for each other. Got it? Except bail. Myron can explain about the bail thing."

Finally, I fell asleep, and what shows up? My bad dream.

It's night. It's raining. I am walking along a lit street. The farther I walk, the farther apart the streetlights are, until I walk past the last one, and all I can see is endless darkness whispering my name. But this time, I follow the whisper deeper and deeper into the blackness. Just as the light behind me disappears, a light appears ahead of me. Then I understand. If I just keep moving, the light I need will find me.

ACKNOWLEDGMENTS

To turn a swirl of words into something as tangible as a book, it takes a lot of talented people. It began with my beta readers, Andrew, Maureen, Linda, Jackie, and Yael. Once recommended changes were incorporated, Kristen of Indigo: Editing, Design, and More fine-tuned each line before it was delivered into the skillful hands of Vinnie for the interior design and Olivia for the cover. They all did their best to create a thing of beauty. Any shortfall is totally on me, the author.

AUTHOR BIO

L. Lee Shaw is the owner of the independent publishing house Boho Books. Through Boho, she has published two novels, *Blood Will Tell*…and *Monster Child*, and co-edited *Analekta*, an anthology of writing. In 2017, in addition to debuting *Aging Out*, she will also debut a relationship book, *Love Imperfect*, and a children's chapter book, *Flunking Magic*, featuring a little witch who is very bad at spells.

www.ingramcontent.com/pod-product-compliance
Lightning Source LLC
Chambersburg PA
CBHW031945130726
47905CB00002BA/659